THE
ACCIDENTAL
WARRIOR

S J MANTLE

Cover Design by Richie Cumberlidge at Daniel Goldsmith Associates Ltd
Typeset by Daniel Goldsmith Associates Ltd, London

The moral right of the author has been asserted.

Matador
9 Priory Business Park,
Wistow Road, Kibworth Beauchamp,
Leicestershire. LE8 0RX
Tel: 0116 279 2299
Email: books@troubador.co.uk
Web: www.troubador.co.uk/matador
Twitter: @matadorbooks

ISBN 978 1789015 171

British Library Cataloguing in Publication Data.
A catalogue record for this book is available from the British Library.

Printed and bound in Great Britain by 4edge Limited

Matador is an imprint of Troubador Publishing Ltd

In memory of my father who inspired my love of history and encouraged me to believe that anything is possible if you are determined enough

PROLOGUE

Philip 11 of Macedon was a remiarkable man. For twenty-three years he ruled Macedonia, transforming it from a primitive, factious kingdom to a centralised, prosperous state. Years of clever political brokering and strategic marriages saw him achieve what Sparta, Athens and Thebes of the fourth and fifth centuries had been unable to: the unification of the Greek States.

In the summer of 336 BC, Philip held a lavish wedding for one of his daughters. The festivities lasted for days. It was an opportunity to show off his wealth and authority to guests who had gathered from across the Greek world. It should have been the start of even greater successes, for he was poised to invade Persia.

As a fitting send-off for the planned invasion of Persia, a dawn ceremony was held to a packed theatre of distinguished spectators, including the King's wives and mistresses and their young children. For all his political clout, Philip also had a reputation as a devoted family man.

As the sun rose that morning, it bathed the theatre in soft golden light. A fanfare announced the start of the ceremony. Expectation filled the air. As the crowd caught sight of the first procession, a roar of approval erupted. Twelve magnificent statues of the gods and a thirteenth, fashioned in the likeness of

1

the King, were carried in. It was a daring show of power. As the King entered the arena, he gestured to his bodyguards to leave his side. Then, as his foot companions fanned out to ensure he was the focus of attention, one of them, a young man called Pausanias, unexpectedly stepped forward and produced a small bladed dagger which he thrust into the King's armpit, unprotected by his armour. As the King fell to the ground, fatally injured, pandemonium broke out.

In the subsequent confusion, Pausanias fled on foot towards the west gate and waiting horses, swiftly pursued by the King's bodyguards. Pausanias would have reached freedom had he not tripped on a root. This mistake cost him his life for he was promptly slain by a spear thrown by one of the bodyguards. This guaranteed there would be no opportunity to question him.

In the days that followed, Macedonia became a dark and perilous place. Precious few believed Pausanias had acted alone. Philip's murder left a power vacuum and although the King's nineteen-year-old son Alexander was quick to assert his claim to the throne and to deal with the ensuing disorder, power games were afoot. Alexander's mother, Olympias, took control of the royal palace. The Macedonian people had little love for her but, as Philip's principle wife, she was now more powerful than ever.

With the main players locked in a battle for power, no-one noticed the King's young children disappear. By the time the alarm was raised it was too late; they had vanished without trace. Despite extensive searching and finger pointing, history offers no clue to their fate.

CHAPTER 1

Detective Harriet Lacey sat at her desk on the third floor of Police Headquarters, in a drab, open-plan office with pale grey walls and 1980s furniture. She was engrossed in cataloguing documents found at the home of an accountant who had died in a blaze, considered suspicious by the Fire Service. Harriet reached for the next item; a smoke-damaged orange note book. Leafing through, she saw page after page of neat, handwritten random numbers, presented in lines of varying lengths. She frowned, trying to understand its content. With no time to study it further, she wrote an exhibit label E61715 and sealed the note book in a clear plastic bag, which she placed on the ever-growing pile on her desk. Harriet paused for a second, for she had the feeling there was more to the accountant's affairs than first met the eye. She made a mental note to investigate further when time allowed. Glancing at the clock on the wall she realised she was going to be late and jumped up, grabbing her jacket as she did so.

As she drove down the road, a call came through on her hands-free from Ben, her fifteen-year-old son.

"Mum, have you washed my sports kit? I need it now."

"No. You were wearing it when Dad took you to Granny and Granddad's on Sunday."

"No, I wasn't."

"Well I think you were, because Dad picked you up from a football match, remember?"

"Shit. Shit. Dad's a cock."

"Ben!" But the phone had gone dead.

It seemed her persona non grata of a husband was about to experience the delights of their hormonal son first-hand. Harriet sighed. She was not going to get involved. She'd been trying hard not to think about Nick.

Conscious of being late for her meeting, Harriet ran up the stairwell to the fourth floor. As she approached Superintendent Alec Brown's office, she paused to catch her breath. The door was slightly ajar. She could hear voices within and leaned in closer to listen; it did not take long to realise she was the topic of conversation.

"... Detective Sergeant Harriet Lacey has to leave Operation Eagle with immediate effect."

"Sir, I don't understand. This is an important enquiry into high-level corruption. Lacey is a key member of the team. It makes absolutely no sense," said Detective Chief Inspector Derek Wynn.

"Look, you don't have to like it, just bloody move her," said Brown.

"Sir, Operation Eagle is a major enquiry. We have only just scratched the surface. The work Harriet and her team are doing in relation to the suspected arson is starting to create some interesting leads."

There was no response from Brown.

"Why would Senior Management even consider moving

one of their most effective detectives from such an important investigation? Harriet Lacey is an outstanding officer; her attention to detail is second to none. She is the most intuitive detective I have ever worked with."

"Wynn, I'm not debating this with you," shouted Brown. "Post her to Operation Chapel. We're not interested in her making a name for herself. Chapel has stalled. There are no active lines of enquiry. It's the ideal place for her to go. She'll have to work for her estranged husband though." Brown was laughing loudly.

Harriet used the wall to steady herself, then, not waiting for a response to her knock, she entered.

"Good morning Superintendent Brown, DCI Wynn."

Brown waved her in. He was busy pouring coffee from an old-fashioned percolator, a chunky, clumsy, pale blue china pot, with a non-descript pattern and large plug. The room was strange, sparsely furnished except the walls, which were plastered with frames containing press releases, certificates, and photographs of her host.

Superintendent Brown plonked a white china cup and saucer into Harriet's hand. His fat little fingers looked remarkably like hairy chipolatas. As Brown sat back in his leather chair, his enormous belly wobbled like a blancmange; his round, fat face flushed by the exertion. It seemed to Harriet he was enjoying himself a little too much. As he leaned forward, the last remaining wisp of hair anchored to his expansive forehead flopped forward.

Wynn cleared his throat and gestured to Harriet to take a seat.

"Harriet, there is no easy way to say this, but you are to leave Operation Eagle with immediate effect." He paused. "I've been ordered to post you to Operation Chapel as of Monday. I guess I don't have to tell you that your husband heads this investigation up? I'm really very sorry."

In the silence Harriet tried to think of an appropriate response. She wondered what she'd done to provoke Senior Management to move her. And, as if she didn't have enough on her plate, she was now expected to work for Nick. To hear his name was bad enough. She bit her lip. What a bloody mess; she could feel her colour rising. She knew better than to cause a scene; she'd been a police officer for twenty years, she knew to protest would be futile.

Finally, Harriet broke the silence. "Well, thank you for having the decency to tell me in person, I appreciate that."

"Good. Well, that's sorted then," said a smirking Brown.

"Harriet, I think it might be helpful to talk this through in my office, if you have a minute?" said Wynn, with his back to Brown.

Harriet nodded and they stood up and left.

Harriet followed Wynn down the five flights of stairs. He looked shorter than his 6 ft. He often seemed to walk with a slight stoop, as if borne down by the cares of the world. His hair was still jet-black even though, she guessed, he must be in his late forties. He was wiry but without the energy one would usually associate with an athletic frame. Harriet liked Wynn; he was steady and competent with a genuine smile and pleasant manner, and he was quite handsome to boot.

In Wynn's office, he shut the door.

"Harriet, please believe me when I say I knew nothing of this until Brown dropped the bombshell just now and, for the record, I completely disagree with the decision. As unprofessional as this is, I do not like, and I do not trust, Brown one little bit."

"Thank you, Sir. It means a lot to have your support. Now what can you tell me about Operation Chapel?"

"I don't know much detail. Apparently there have been a series of unexplained deaths across the country, with startling similarities. The victims are high-profile and respected pillars of the community. A professor, a hospital consultant, a barrister, an accountant, a company director and, I believe, a scientist. All males, in their fifties or older. None appear to have had pre-existing significant health issues, or financial worries."

"Did any of them know each other?"

"As far as can be ascertained, no. Our team are liaising with the other police forces involved. The pathologists have so far failed to find a cause of death. There are no obvious signs of trauma, no signs of violence, no signs of a struggle."

"So why does the team think the deaths are suspicious and linked?"

"All were found lying on their backs with their hands folded across their chests. Their eyes had been closed. They appear to have been deliberately placed in this position, and each had been tattooed, post-mortem."

"Tattooed?" Harriet was now sitting on the edge of her chair.

"Yes. Identical tattoos of a snake, possibly a viper."

"A snake?" Harriet shuddered.

"Yes, tattooed onto the underside of the upper left arm."

"In every case?"

"As far as I know."

"And do we know the significance of this?"

"Sadly, no. But I will ask Detective Sergeant Steve Smith to bring you up to speed. He can help smooth your transition to the team. There is a briefing at eight a.m. on Monday morning. Good luck, Harriet, and please know that I am here if you need anything."

"Thank you, Sir, I appreciate that," she said, shaking Wynn's hand. She turned to go.

"Oh, and Harriet, just one more thing. I probably shouldn't tell you this, but the expectation is that you will lie low on Operation Chapel."

CHAPTER 2

Harriet had every intention of leaving the building, but as she reached the door to the car park, she changed her mind. She did not usually shy away from difficult situations but this was different; it was personal. Taking a deep breath, she turned and entered Operation Chapel.

It was late in the day and the incident room was deserted except for Nick who was at his desk in a small, glass-walled office at the far end of the room.

Professionally, Nick was a well-respected Senior Investigating Officer: experienced, intuitive, and generally viewed as fair and honourable. She had fallen in love with this 6 ft 2, blond, bearded, bear of a man. But it hadn't taken her long to realise that he liked to be noticed.

Harriet knocked on the open door. Nick looked up in surprise, jumping to his feet.

"Harry. You're the last person I expected to see tonight. Come in, and no, before you ask, I had nothing to do with your move. In fact, I've just finished speaking to Alec Brown about it."

"Really?" Harriet folded her arms.

"Yes. It didn't go well, I'm afraid. I told him that moving you to my team was at best insensitive and at worst vindictive. But he just grinned from behind his desk. The smug bastard seemed to be rather enjoying himself."

"Did he say anything else?"

"*Sorry old boy, but it's been decided at a much higher level than you or I, so like it or not, you have no say in the matter,*" said Nick, mimicking Brown.

"To which you said?"

"Alec, please don't piss me off any more than you have already. You'll have to do better than that."

"Did you say that, or shout that?" Harriet coloured.

Nick shot her a look. "I may have raised my voice a little."

"And then what?"

"Nothing much," Nick replied too quickly.

"Didn't you ask him where the order came from, or the reason for it? Or even why Operation Chapel?"

"Well, of course I did." Nick's voice was still raised. Harriet thought he looked flushed.

"His lame response was to say something like, '*Look old boy. I really am not at liberty to say. I followed my orders, and I really don't know myself.*'"

"And you let it go at that?" said Harriet, hands on hips.

"No. Brown offered to make representations on my behalf and report back," said a defensive Nick. "I told him that he'd better do more than that, that I wanted a conversation with someone in the know, or I promised him there would be consequences." Nick was pacing up and down the small office. He turned to face her, but Harriet avoided his gaze.

"Look Harry, I'm sorry. I'm sorry about your job. I'm sorry about the fact you now must work with me. In fact, I'm sorry about everything. I made a mistake."

"Stop." Harriet raised her hand.

"Have you read my letters yet?"

"I can't do this right now. Not yet. I'm not ready. So, please, if you hear anything from Brown, let me know?"

"Of course," came his whispered reply, as Harriet strode out of the office, no nearer to the truth.

She sat in the car, she did not know for how long; she needed to compose herself, her whole body was shaking.

Returning home, Harriet entered the house she had once loved so much. She made her way through the black and white tiled entrance hall to the kitchen at the rear of the property. French doors at the far end of the room opened onto a sheltered courtyard. Head pounding, and body aching, she slipped off her boots and poured herself an enormous glass of red wine. Collapsing onto the sofa, she stretched out. Reaching behind her head for the iPod, she pressed the 'play' button. Phil Collins blasted out Separate Lives and she began to weep in earnest. She missed having the children around, she missed the chaos of family life, she missed not feeling angry, hurt and tired. Wiping her tears with a tissue from her pocket, she picked up the landline.

"Annie, it's Harriet, is this a convenient time?"

"Harry, how lovely to hear from you. Yes, of course. You've been on my mind, haven't heard from you for a while. What's up?"

"How do you know anything's up? I've not said anything yet."

"You forget I've known you an awful long time, I can tell by the tone of your voice, and besides I can hear you sniffing."

"You can?"

"Yep. Now, why do you sound so sad?"

"Oh, I don't know, it's just, everything's such a mess. Annie, I didn't ring to burden you with my problems, I just wanted to hear a friendly voice."

"What are friends for, if not to be here when things get tough? Come on, grab another tissue and tell me what's on your mind."

"Thanks, Annie, but I don't actually know where to start; I just feel really low."

"Yes, but you aren't the sort of person to get down without good reason, so what's going on?"

"Um, one lunchtime about six weeks ago, I popped back home to pick up some clothes for the dry cleaners. As I ran upstairs I thought I heard a giggle. The door to our bedroom was slightly ajar so I went to investigate. I popped my head round the door frame and, and, oh ..."

"Hey, Harry, stop. You don't have to tell me anything you don't want to."

"No, no, I need to tell someone. I've been going mad trying to make sense of it all. So, there's my naked husband shagging some tart in our bed."

"Bloody hell, Harry."

"I know, but it was my reaction which scares me the most. I still can't believe I'm capable of such rage. I feel totally ashamed."

"I'm pretty sure you don't need to."

"It still seems a bit surreal. You see, I just began to scream..."

"Yes, and I'd say: Well done you."

"But then I launched myself at him. By now he was standing by the foot of the bed clutching a pillow to his bits. And..."

"It's okay. Take a deep breath. Take more time, if you need to."

"So, I ran at him... and punched him in the chest as well as the face."

"What did he do?"

"That's just it, he did nothing, said nothing, not once did he try to protect himself, just stood there naked still clutching the bloody pillow with tears rolling down his cheeks. This only seemed to fuel my rage. Then as suddenly as it arrived, the fury subsided, and I ran to the bathroom to throw up. When I came out he'd gone to his parents. I found a note in the kitchen."

"Well, it sounds as if he got off lightly."

"Not really Annie, I made a real mess of his face; the first of the bruising was visible even before I'd thrown the last punch..."

"Well, I'd say he deserved it."

"No, no, he really didn't. What he did was wrong, yes, it broke my heart. But my reaction was out of order. I've spent the best part of my adult life trying to be the best police officer I can be, striving to make a difference to people's lives. For God's sake, I even spent five years on the Domestic Abuse Unit, dealing with men and women who suffered terribly at the hands of their partners and now I'm as guilty as those I helped to prosecute. I feel so embarrassed, so mortified by my behaviour. How can I honestly continue as a police officer? In truth, I think the only way forward is to confess to my current boss Chief Inspector Derek Wynn..."

"No, no, you bloody don't, stop this now! Stop beating yourself up. You reacted the way you did because your world fell apart around you. Nick could easily have put an end to it, but chose not to. Don't do this, please."

"I just don't know..."

"I'll let you into a little secret, Harriet Lacey: you are human, and as such you have foibles and faults and flaws just like the rest of us. None of us are perfect. It's that we learn from our mistakes that's important."

"I suppose."

"What has Nick said about what happened?"

"We've not talked about it."

"What, not at all?"

"Nope."

"What about the children, are they okay?"

"Thankfully, they seem remarkably indifferent. They know Nick and I have had a fight, but they don't seem too stressed by it, they probably assume things will blow over. Our lives have been rather dislocated recently. I've been working punishingly long hours and had most of my rest days cancelled. Nick's situation has been less intense but has still resulted in some long shifts. It came to a head when Ben and Amelia came to us to say they'd had enough of waiting in the cold to be picked up long after everyone else had gone home, of being palmed off on family friends, of late-night meals and the lack of instant help with their homework. It was their suggestion that they de-camp to Nick's parents during the school week. So now they flit backwards and forwards between addresses depending on who's around."

"Your kids are smart and self-confident."

"They are, but believe me they still have their moments."

"I'm sure."

"I went to see Nick today."

"Really?"

"Yes, it's been a shit day; I got told this afternoon that with immediate effect I'm to leave the incident room I've been working on all these months, for another. Only problem is that this room is headed up by Nick."

"No way, no way, they can't do that, can they?"

"Annie, they can do what they like, it actually happens quite a lot."

"What, estranged couples being expected to work together?"

"Yes. It is mean and insensitive, but we are basically expected to be professional about it and get on with it."

"I find that really, really disturbing."

"Anyway, as I mentioned, I went to see Nick. My desire to find out why I'd been moved outweighed my reluctance to speak with him, just, but as it turns out, although angry at the decision, he didn't seem to know any more than I did. It was hard though. I couldn't look him in the eye; a couple of times I felt myself getting emotional and I felt nauseous throughout. But I did it."

"Well done girl."

"Annie, I just don't know if I have the strength to take up this new posting. I look in the mirror and I don't recognise the woman staring back at me. I've lost sense of who I am. I'm finding it difficult to cope. Little things I usually take in my stride seem overwhelming."

"What do you mean?"

"I thought I had it sussed: two lovely children, a handsome and successful husband, a career that made a difference. I saw myself as a smart professional woman in control of her life. But now when I look in the mirror I just see a tired, frumpy, broken face staring back, a woman who has to deal with daily gossip and innuendo and who doesn't have a clue whether she can be bothered to claw her way out of the big black hole that is threatening to engulf her..."

"Oh Harry, my darling, please don't cry. I'd no idea you were so down. You need to listen to me very carefully: you are smart and professional. A truly beautiful woman with an incredible smile. Astonishingly caring and bright, and witty too. And you are today's news; next week, someone else will be the focus of the gossips."

"Thank you, Annie, I've got myself into quite a state."

"Harry, you are the strongest woman I know. It seems to me you could really do with some time to yourself. It would help you to come to terms with what's happened, give yourself some time to get your head together."

"I really don't think I can. What about the children? My new job? And poor old Dad? I'm so worried about him, and Mum is exhausted. His condition is deteriorating. No, I really can't."

"Harry, you can make as many excuses as you like, but you can't carry on as you are. The children are fine with their Dad and his parents, the job can wait a week and you are unlikely to be much help or indeed comfort to your parents in this state."

"Okay, okay, I submit. Thank you for listening to me and for being there for me."

"You're most welcome, now go and take care of yourself. You will soon bounce back, you know."

Harriet sat in the dark and thought about her situation, mulling over her conversation with Annie. It didn't take her long to realise that Annie was right, she did need time to consider her life.

She reached again for the phone.

"Hello?" said a familiar male voice, clearing his throat.

"Sir, it's Harriet. So sorry to ring you at home and so late on a Friday evening…"

"It's not a problem, what can I do for you?" Derek Wynn spoke softly, almost as if he'd picked up on Harriet's vulnerability. Harriet blushed in the darkness.

"Well, as you are still technically my line manager, is there any chance I can take a few days' leave? I need to get my head together and sort out some personal issues before I start Operation Chapel."

"I think that's a good idea. I'm happy to authorise it. I'll tell Nick I've tasked you with a sensitive piece of work and I can't spare you until it's completed. I'll tell him that you'll be starting Chapel a week on Monday. How does that sound?"

"That's great, thank you so much."

"See you in a week," he said kindly.

CHAPTER 3

A fortnight earlier

Kate Squire's focus was a doorway to a non-descript grey building opposite. In the early morning chill, she rubbed her hands together and waited.

An hour later, she emerged from the shadows the moment she spotted the white Range Rover Sport drive off. Kate moved quickly and soon her battered grey Golf was following at a safe distance. After several miles, the Range Rover turned left off the High Street, but just as Kate approached the lights, they turned red.

"Oh, for God's sake, you're joking, bloody hell!" she shouted, slamming her hands on the dashboard.

When the lights changed again, the vehicle was nowhere to be seen. She drove up and down several residential roads, but there was no sign of it. She was perspiring, the sound of her racing heart deafening in her ears.

"Where the hell are you, Cleo? Come on, where are you?"

A minute or two later, Kate's Golf turned into Highland Avenue, announcing its presence with its noisy exhaust. She knew she should get it fixed. Spotting the stationary Range Rover, she parked and leapt out of her car.

But she was unsure where to start her search. She guessed she did not have much time, she was sure Cleo was there to kill.

Her best chance must lie in concentrating on the houses on the same side of the road as Cleo's car, but would Cleo really be so arrogant as to park her car close to the scene of the crime? The street was empty, there was no-one to ask. She ran from house to house peering through front windows, hoping against hope she would find the one she was looking for. Her search was becoming farcical. A post van pulled into the top of the road.

Kate ran towards the unsuspecting postman. Breathless, she managed to gasp, "Really sorry to bother you, but can you tell me where Professor Martin Grey lives please?"

"Number 42, love, the one with the green door."

"Thank you," shouted Kate over her shoulder as she sped towards the house.

Cleo's car was indeed parked outside. Kate rang the doorbell and hammered on the door. She peered into the front window, but it was dark within. She could see no movement. Flustered, she ran back to the road, then back to the house. Not willing to give up yet, she pounded the door. Looking around for inspiration she spotted a stone tortoise in the flower bed. Picking it up, she glanced around before stepping into the porch and striking the glass panel in the door. It cracked; she struck it again and again until she'd made a large enough hole to safely put her hand through. Feeling for the latch she managed to flick it up into the open position before trying the handle. To her immense relief, the door opened.

"Hello, anyone there? Hello, Professor Grey?" There was no reply. The hallmark of an expensive perfume hung in the air, heavy notes of jasmine and rose. It did not take her long to locate the Professor in his office, at the back of the Edwardian town house.

He was tied to a chair. Kate rushed across. Kneeling at his feet she looked for signs of breathing but there were none. Placing her fingers on his neck she felt for a pulse; his skin was still warm to the touch. Trembling now, she tried over and over, but she couldn't find a pulse. Breathless, she grabbed the Professor by the shoulders.

"Wake up Professor. Please wake up! Fuck! Fuck." Cleo had thwarted her.

Kate sat with her back against a bookshelf. She closed her eyes and took a deep breath. Poor Professor Grey, what a waste of life, what a tragedy. Opening her eyes, she surveyed his wrinkled features. His neatly cut white hair, his freshly shaven face, save for a few long hairs lining the top of his cheeks. As she stood up she spotted his reading glasses resting on the desk. Glasses he would never have use for again. She felt her stomach tighten.

"Oh God, what do I do? This is such a mess."

Hastily untying the Professor, she laid him out on the floor, closing his eyes and placing his hands on his chest in the age-old tradition. As she adjusted his tweed jacket, she detected something hard in the left breast pocket. Cautiously, she slipped her hand inside and pulled out an old pocket tape recorder. Examining it closer, she stopped the tape and re-wound it, before pressing 'play'.

"I knew immediately I saw you that it was fruitless to struggle. You are very clearly in your prime. I'm no match for your youth," said a male voice, which Kate assumed was the Professor, although they had never met.

There was silence. *"I know why you're here. To an extent I've been anticipating this day."* Still no response.

"Antiphanes wisely once stated, 'The quest for riches darkens the sense of right and wrong.'"

"Who the hell is Antiphanes? And what the hell is that supposed to mean?" snapped a woman's voice. Cleo.

Seemingly undaunted, the Professor replied, *"Antiphanes was an ancient Greek dramatist. I will leave you to ponder the meaning of his words, but let's just be clear, what you are about to do is profoundly sinful."*

There was a short pause before he continued. *"I know why you've come, I've asked too many awkward questions, ruffled too many feathers, and become a nuisance that must be silenced. It's no good shooting me that dark look with those luminous green eyes. I don't scare easily. And a word of warning or maybe even wisdom. I advise you to think long and hard about what you are doing. Though I suspect from your poise I am by no means your first victim. I doubt, however, it's possible to persist in this line of work without it taking its emotional toll. Unless of course you truly believe in the justness of your cause or you are just emotionally immature. Is that what you are, emotionally immature?"*

"*Shut up, will you? Just shut up! You know I'm trying hard not to listen to you. You are by far the most annoying man I've come across in a long time.*" There was real menace in Cleo's voice.

"*To take the life of an innocent man is to commit the ultimate sin. No doubt you will be handsomely rewarded for your efforts. But you will never be free from your murderous actions. They will haunt you and gnaw at your conscience for the rest of your life.*"

"*That's enough!*" Cleo yelled. This was followed by a loud shout from the Professor, then some muffled sounds, which Kate could not make out. She wondered perhaps if Cleo had put her hand over the Professor's mouth to silence him.

But Professor Grey wasn't finished yet; in a much-subdued voice he began to describe his predicament. "*There's a strange numbness coursing through my body, it started in my fingers and toes but it's quickly spreading to my legs and arms.*" Then silence. Kate noted little emotion in his voice, his analytical mind appeared to have kicked in.

Just as Kate was about to stop the tape, the Professor started to talk again. "*The numbness is moving at an alarming rate. My chest is tight; it's getting much harder to breathe. I'm having difficulty focussing now, my vision is becoming blurred, I really can't catch my breath...*"

There was to be no further dialogue from the Professor, just a series of laboured noises which, Kate guessed, were the Professor's last strenuous efforts to breathe.

It was a few minutes before Kate felt able to resume; the recording had left her flushed and tearful. She turned to the man now lying at her feet.

"I promise you, Professor, I will do my utmost to get you justice. I'm so sorry I failed you."

As she turned to leave, she hesitated for a moment, before kneeling at the Professor's side and tenderly kissing his forehead.

Placing the tape recorder in her jacket pocket, she left via the patio doors at the back of the house; the garden gate led to an adjacent road.

Predictably, there was no sign of the Range Rover when Kate reached her car. She drove off, only stopping when she was some distance from Highfield Avenue. Flushed and shaking, she made a call on her mobile.

"Dad, oh Dad, I've... I don't. I don't know how to... Oh, God..."

"It's okay, take a deep breath and blow your nose, take your time."

"Dad, I'm so, so out of my depth..." sobbed Kate.

"It's okay, now slow down, take your time."

"Promise you won't be too mad?"

"I'm sure it can't be that bad, Kate."

"Promise!"

"Okay, I promise."

"A couple of months ago at work, I almost walked in on her."

"Who?"

"Cleo Morris; she didn't see me, but she'd not changed, still a bully."

"Oh God, Kate."

"I know, anyway, it seems there was a fault on her laptop and she was insistent that the repair be expedited, offered to pay over the odds for it. She also wanted a security upgrade installed."

"Right? So?"

"Well, I couldn't resist, I just had to look."

"You didn't!"

"I did. After all, security networking is my thing."

"I feel a 'but' coming."

"Well, I found some very cryptic deleted emails. I became convinced that Cleo is involved in... this may seem crazy but, in murder. When I discovered references to the Guardians I didn't know what to do, only that I couldn't go to the police without proof, so I decided to follow her in my down time."

"Murder? Really?"

"Yes!"

"Good God, Kate!"

"Dad, you promised, you wouldn't get angry." Kate began to sob again.

"Okay, I'm sorry, carry on," he said more softly.

"Stupidly, I followed her car today, but I lost her, and by the time I found the address and forced entry... he was dead. And she was gone."

"Who was dead?"

"Professor Martin Grey."

"Martin Grey? How did you know he was the target?"

"It was a guess, I'd seen his name highlighted on her computer."

"And how do you know Cleo was responsible for his death?"

"Because he recorded the whole thing on his tape recorder, which I now have."

"So, let me recap, you follow and lose Cleo, force entry to a house, where you find a dead Professor and a tape recording of his death?"

"Yes, pretty much."

"So, of course you called the police and told them all this, made a statement and handed over the tape recorder?"

"Um, no not exactly, Dad, I panicked. I thought I would be blamed, I'm so stupid."

It took a good few moments for Kate's Dad to respond.

"Well, I'd say you are potentially in considerable trouble and before you jump down my throat, I'm not judging you. Let me think."

" I knew you'd know what to do." Kate blew her nose.

"Okay, Cleo is bad news. I think you can safely assume that she will be aware of your surveillance of her. From what you've said, she will have heard your attempts to get the Professor's attention. She could cause trouble for you. On the other hand, you have the Professor's tape recorder which is evidence of her involvement. Where did you find it? And, did the recording give any indication of how the Professor died?"

"Um, it was in his breast pocket. He described what was

happening to him in an analytical way; dizziness, breathlessness, but there was no gun shot or anything obvious like that."

"Okay, so Cleo was probably unaware of its existence. And the tape was still recording when you found it?"

"Oh, my God, yes! Oh Dad, what am I going to do?"

"Well, I'm guessing that you are not identifiable in any way on the tape, But, and it's a very big but, you've interfered with a crime scene, not only by moving the body, but by taking the tape recorder, which is a very serious matter. A quick question, did you take any measures to cover your tracks at the house?"

"What do you mean?"

"Tidy up, wipe down surfaces, door handles etc?"

"No, I was so upset and anxious that I might be discovered, I fled the house as soon as I could."

"Well, in that case I'd say there is a very good chance that your DNA will be at the scene."

"Oh God, Dad, what am I going to do? Are you going to turn me into the police?" Kate wailed.

"Oh Katie, no I'm not, but I do need you to tell me why you got yourself involved in this after you were explicitly advised against going it alone?"

"Um, that's something I've been asking myself, over and over, and it's hard to put into words... Um, it was more of a feeling than a thought process. I felt compelled, or obliged if you like; can you understand that?"

"Yes, you are undoubtedly your mother's daughter, but if she were here today she'd be disappointed that you either didn't comprehend the rules laid down for you, or you simply chose to ignore them. Is what I'm saying making sense to you? It's very important that it does."

"An obligation not just to myself but to others?"

"Yes, exactly. Now as far as I can see there is only one course of action open to you and you must hope that they are prepared to help you."

"Thank you, thank you so much. Will I be summoned? Or should I contact them?"

"Oh, they will be in touch with you. In the meantime, keep a low profile and try not to stress too much. Remember, I love you and I'm proud of you. For you do have a strong moral compass, you just need to learn to read it better. And do me a favour, stay away from Cleo."

CHAPTER 4

Harriet woke early; it was the first time in a long time she'd had a Saturday off work. Feeling drained and tired, she made herself a pot of coffee and breakfasted on brown toast and homemade marmalade. Feeling brighter, she decided it was time to take a long hard look at herself, literally. Standing in front of her full-length mirror, she was determined not to be despondent. She was tall at 5 ft 11, but with a slim and shapely figure. "Not bad for a thirty-eight-year-old," she mused; new bras would help to lift her figure. She turned her attention to her hair. Long, straight and mid-brown, it looked a bit dull and tired, but nothing that a colour and cut couldn't remedy. Next, she concentrated on her face: an eyebrow re-shape and new make-up would even out her skin tone and help to ensure her deep green eyes looked more prominent. Then: a review of her wardrobe. Out went several tired trouser suits, practical for work but not particularly feminine or inspiring.

She showered and changed and went to meet Ben and Amelia for lunch in town. Her children were waiting for her, she could see them at a window seat in the pizza restaurant as she approached. Ben was in his trademark black jeans and T-shirt, his mop of dark hair obscuring much of his face. Harriet wondered when or even if his fascination with

American Rock would end. And Amelia, lovely Amelia, enthusiastic and sunny, only a couple of years younger than Ben but what a difference that made. At thirteen, there was just a hint that her body was changing, specifically the little bumps on her chest, but she was still blissfully unsophisticated and seemingly untouched by the latest teenage crazes. There she was with her long mane of untamed red curls tumbling over her freckled face, wearing jeans and a top that was far too short.

She's grown again, thought Harriet, as she waved enthusiastically. Amelia waved back. Ben just rolled his eyes at his mother.

After lunch, they went shopping for trainers and CDs before Ben and Amelia left to meet their Dad. It was then that Harriet took the opportunity to throw herself into some serious shopping. Ably assisted by an energetic twenty-something assistant, she overhauled her wardrobe with feminine dresses, tunics, leggings, new knickers and bras, heeled boots and new make-up. There was just time for a trip to the local nail bar.

On the Monday, Harriet chose a new short cropped blonde haircut followed by an eyebrow reshape on her way home. Her transformation was complete. That evening, as she stood in front of the mirror in one of her new outfits, she felt pleased with the result.

It was nearly 11.30 a.m. on Tuesday when Harriet drove down the steep hill into the sleepy seaside village of Aberporth in West Wales, about ten miles south west of New

Quay. The sun was shining and it was unseasonably warm. As she descended the hill, Harriet could make out the odd sailing boat in the bay below. She wound down the window and filled her nostrils with the cool salty sea air, smiling with pleasure. Slowly, she negotiated the car down a narrow lane, bordered by an ancient lichen-stained stone wall. Less than 200 metres along, she turned left through a gateway and onto a stony yard. There in front of her stood a small white-washed cottage. She quickly found the key under the dustbin and let herself into the main room. It smelt musty and stale, so she set about opening the upstairs windows. Next, she brought in her bag and set it down on the table. It contained a pile of unopened letters from Nick.

After getting some supplies from the village shop, she made herself a large cheese and tomato sandwich. She ate this hungrily at the wooden picnic table, at the top of the tiny garden gazing out over the bay below. She closed her eyes; a slight breeze caressed her hair and the sun's warmth kissed her face. For the first time in many weeks Harriet felt more positive; the cloak of despair slowly seemed to be lifting.

In the distance, she could hear the familiar sound of families on the beach; closer still was the sound of hungry gulls. Harriet felt a sudden and intense sense of relief from the stress of the last few weeks. She had longed to escape, to get away from the everyday and have time to reflect. For in truth she had barely been able to hold it together.

After lunch, she went for a walk, Nick's letters tucked under her arm, to a favourite bench perched on the edge of the cliff.

From here she could survey both bays, which were separated by an outcrop of rock known locally as the 'point'. The tide was just beginning to turn, and she watched as small children's spades battled unsuccessfully to defeat the advancing tide.

Harriet was inclined to believe Nick when he had promised that the 'incident' was the first and only sexual encounter he'd had in their marriage. She knew that he was probably hurting as much as she was, and consumed with regret. But as she reached for his letters she wondered if it was even possible for a relationship to fully recover from such betrayal. She didn't doubt that he was embarrassed, that he was guilt-laden. Nor did she doubt that he had not set out to hurt her, and yet he was a grown man, who could so easily have made different choices. She set about reading the letters.

Glancing down at Nick's last letter, she read and reread the same passage over and over.

You are always in my thoughts, because I adore you· I feel truly bereft· I have lost my best friend, my lover, my wife and my confidante· I yearn to lie in your arms again, to laugh with you, to touch you, but I fear I have lost you forever, and I am truly broken-hearted· I don't know what to do, where to turn; what is the future without you? Each time I catch a glimpse of you, I feel pain in my chest and I am filled with despair· If only I could make this right· Still, please know that I love you now and for all time; you are a truly gracious, kind and beautiful woman·

Harriet took a deep breath. No, it was no good, she wasn't ready to forgive, wasn't ready to consider the future. In truth, she found Nick's letters self-indulgent. He was good at talking about how acutely he was hurting, but not so good at recognising how she might be feeling. Gathering up the letters she walked down a steep pathway to the beach. Rolling up her jeans, she removed her shoes and socks before walking onto the warm sand. As she wiggled her toes, the powdery sand trickled through and made her smile. Placing the pile of letters under her shoes, she made her way to the water's edge and began to pick up small shells from the shoreline, something she'd done many times before. Once her pockets were full, she spent a peaceful half hour exploring the rock pools, before heading back to the cottage. As she made her way up the slate slope, she glanced across the beach to the car park opposite. She could see a man with binoculars looking in her direction. His binoculars seemed to be trained on her. She shook her head, he was probably just admiring the bay.

That evening Harriet sat in the sheltered front porch of the cottage to admire the sunset. She had just finished a plate of pasta when her mobile sounded. It was Amelia.

"Ben is being a real bastard, Mum." On this occasion, Harriet decided not to pull her daughter up on her language. She sounded upset.

"He keeps telling everyone I'm fat and making nasty comments when I have a snack, like '*That won't do your stretch marks any good*.'" Or he just snorts like a pig. I'm fed up with it, I hate him, he always puts me down in front of his friends and in front of mine."

"Have you told him how it makes you feel, that it hurts your feelings?"

"What do you think?" snapped Amelia. "He just laughs and makes jokes about whales and their blubber."

"Amelia, don't take your frustration out on me, please," said Harriet sternly. "I'll speak to Ben and to Granny."

"Okay, thanks Mum," said Amelia, sounding immediately brighter. "Love you. I'm off to see Georgia now."

"I love you too." And that was that.

It felt so good to have space, time to think. For a while, she'd felt there was a danger her low mood would overwhelm her. She had even contemplated running away, but that was not who Harriet Lacey was, and that was not what she did.

CHAPTER 5

Kate was having a dilemma about what to wear. She understood first impressions mattered, and she was in no doubt that she was in trouble with the Guardians for acting on her own and 'off script'. She wanted to make a good impression, not look too frivolous, too sexy, or indeed too young and inexperienced. She decided on a navy trouser suit and white shirt.

She walked down the worn stone steps into the basement of the commanding building, fully aware of her churning stomach, pounding heart and quick breathing.

Reluctantly, she entered an anteroom, where she was met by a smart man, perhaps in his late fifties, it was hard to tell. He was tall and athletic and still quite handsome, but the light was poor and she could not really get the measure of him. He smiled and beckoned her to follow. They walked down a long, poorly lit wooden panelled corridor and entered a vast room at the far end. This was also wood panelled. In the middle of the room stood a gigantic heavy wooden table, around which thirty or more individuals were seated. At the head of the table closest to the door and with his back to her was the Custodian.

"Kate, please come in, take a seat." The Custodian pointed to a seat on his right about halfway down the vast table.

But Kate had stopped in her tracks.

"Dad?"

"Yes, Kate."

"You're the Custodian?" she exclaimed.

"Yes."

Kate's hand shot up to her mouth; a small squeal escaped.

"Kate, please take your seat. You've been invited here today to explain your recent actions. We have to decide whether we can, or indeed should, assist you or whether to take sanctions against you." He paused for a moment, choosing his words carefully.

"Kate, we accept that what you did, you did without malice, but our rules have been in place for well over two thousand years. So, it's puzzling to us all why you chose to breach them. And what exactly you expected to achieve?"

Kate stood up, smoothed her jacket, and placed her hands lightly on the table, partly to help balance her, but also to stop them from shaking. She took a deep breath.

"Senior Guardians, I'm grateful to you for allowing me to address you today. Unfortunately, although I'm intelligent, I often act rashly and the situation I find myself in is a prime example of that. We live in extraordinary times and, whilst I understand the sanctity of our rules, I will admit that they did not occur to me at the time I decided to follow Cleo Morris. I was thoughtless and impulsive, for I realise now that not only have I let myself down, but all of you..."

"After your recent antics, you'll be lucky to remain a member of this family at all, silly girl," shouted an elderly female opposite, wagging her bony index finger in Kate's direction.

"That's enough, please show some respect," instructed the Custodian. "Continue, Kate."

"I was going to say, I would like to apologise unequivocally to you all for my arrogance and thoughtlessness, and beg your forgiveness. And this is not an excuse for my actions, but I would like to say that life today is immeasurably different to the era in which the Guardians were founded. We were created out of turmoil, from the ruins of a great kingdom, where jealousy and cruelty had the upper hand. We ourselves haven't always played by the rules, for in our very inception our ancestors were forced to outwit the King's enemies. Was it not they who refused to stand by and allow the King's family to perish? Did they not do their level best to stand up for what they believed to be right as well as follow the wishes of their King?"

"So, you think you are special because of your blood line, that you have a calling? And as such, should be rewarded as a heroine for your meddling, do you?" asked a woman on the other side of the table.

"No, not at all, I was just trying to point out that sometimes it may be okay to bend the rules a bit for the greater good." Kate sighed. This was so much harder than she could have imagined.

A wizened male to her left glared at her. "So what is your justification for what you've done then? Because I'm having difficulty understanding why you couldn't just let things be.

This is not your fight alone." This was followed by a series of nods from around the table, and whispered mutterings from the woman next to her.

Kate hadn't anticipated this level of hostility, but before she could answer, a man wearing a smart green tweed three-piece suit and holding a cane got to his feet.

"Guardians, can I suggest that we all take a long hard look at ourselves? It's easy to be smug when all we do is sit here week after week, year after year. How many empty seats are there? I can count at least ten. Could it not be argued that we have failed in our duty? That essentially we've allowed our fellow members to perish without any concerted attempt to intervene…"

The room ignited. It took the Custodian to return order.

"Fellow Guardians, that's enough! Cyrus, please continue, but I urge caution."

"Well, I was going to say that whilst I agree Kate's actions were reckless and thoughtless, her motives were honourable. Surely you can all recall your early twenties? I can, and I'm sure like me at times you were impatient, rash, with a sense of invincibility. We all made mistakes, it's part of learning our craft. I see much of her mother in her and we would not have survived, had it not been for her tenacity and bravery. I still miss her terribly. So, I'm just saying I think that instead of berating Kate we could perhaps consider helping her?"

Kate sat in silence, her head bowed. She had not anticipated that there might be a friendly face in the room.

"Kate, I think it might help if you play the Professor's recording," said Cyrus kindly.

Kate produced the tape recorder from her pocket and turned the volume up to its maximum, before placing it on the table and pressing the 'play' button. The room fell silent. When it had finished, no-one spoke. Some, however, appeared visibly upset by what they'd heard.

Kate sat down and looked at her lap. She felt dejected. After what seemed like an age, the Custodian spoke.

"Thank you, Kate, for your honesty; we now need to talk about this and make some decisions. Everyone, I think it's time we had a break. Be back in twenty minutes please. Kate, please stay behind and see me for a minute, will you?"

Once everyone had filed out, Kate's father smiled at her.

"Well done, you conducted yourself with dignity. I'm sorry if my presence here startled you, it was not my intention, but the rules did not allow me to tell you earlier."

"Oh Dad, I had no idea,.When? How?"

"Can we talk about it later?"

Kate nodded.

"What I will say is that I owe the Guardians my sanity, for they stepped in and took care of us when your mother died. Without their kindness and compassion, I'm not sure what would have happened. Now, the tape recorder needs to go to the police. It's one thing to alter a crime scene, but it's totally another to remove evidence. Send it to the Senior Investigating Officer, Superintendent Nick Lacey at George Street Police Station."

Kate nodded. Her father took her hand in his and gave it a reassuring squeeze before she was escorted out of the building and back into the spring sunshine.

CHAPTER 6

Harriet arrived home on Saturday afternoon and unpacked. But it wasn't until she went to make a cup of tea that she noticed the door to the garden was open. She took a step backwards; initial disbelief was replaced by anger at the intrusion into her home. Forensically aware, she took care where she trod and what she touched. Closer inspection of the door suggested it had been forced, there were tool marks on the wood and around the locking mechanism. Inside, Harriet found a broken vase in the lounge, the contents of her jewellery box on the sofa in the master bedroom and clothes strewn over the bedroom floor. There appeared to have been no attempt to remove any of the high-value electrical items, such as televisions or computers.

Harriet called the Police Control Room. A Community Officer arrived, followed by Scenes of Crime. She'd not expected such service, but it seemed burglary was a current force priority. As she watched the Scenes of Crime officer work, she pondered the fact that considerable effort had gone into breaking in, for so little to be disturbed. It almost seemed staged, and she was left with an uneasy feeling in the pit of her stomach. Out of courtesy, she telephoned Nick.

"I need to come and have a look," he said, sounding concerned.

"You don't need to do anything, I have it under control."

Five minutes later Nick appeared, looking slightly dishevelled. Harriet was at the top of the steps to the house waiting for him. He flashed her a smile.

"Nice hair," he said, as he followed her into the hallway.

Nick wandered from room to room with Harriet shadowing him. She saw that occasionally he took a swig from a hip flask, but only when he thought he was alone. After about an hour, he had finished.

"Look, this is going to sound lame, but I'm uneasy about this, I don't want you living here alone."

"I'm absolutely fine." She looked at him, arms folded.

"I know you think you are, but please, I'm worried."

"Well, if you give me a compelling argument for your uneasiness then I might consider going to stay with a friend, but if not, then I'm staying put."

Harriet noticed Nick shifting his weight from one foot to another, he looked uncomfortable but didn't raise the topic again.

Monday morning arrived all too soon; Harriet's first day on Operation Chapel. Feeling nauseous, she paused before taking a deep breath and pushing open the door. The room was teeming with officers and staff; some were drinking coffee and tea, chatting and laughing; some were on computers, others on their mobile phones. For an instant, everyone stopped to stare at the glamorous woman in the doorway. An awkward silence followed, before a tall, slightly gangly man in a grey suit, with a mop of black unruly hair and dark goatee beard, launched himself across the room towards her.

"Hello, Harriet, I'm Detective Sergeant Steve Smith. It's good to meet you."

Harriet noted his smart and athletic appearance, guessing he was probably in his late thirties.

"Thank you, good to meet you too."

"Your reputation precedes you," he said, immediately looking alarmed and blushing wildly. "Oh, I didn't mean it like that. God, sorry, embarrassing."

Despite herself, Harriet broke into a smile.

Harriet was used to moving from one job to another at short notice but this was different. For the first time in her career she felt unsure of herself.

Three days were set aside to allow her to familiarise herself with the investigation. After that, the plan was for her to meet her team and to start work in earnest. As Harriet prepared to get herself up to speed she tried to put the prospect of the Friday's Senior Investigating Team briefings out of her mind. She knew she'd have to work hard to be able to make a useful contribution and to have any chance of being accepted by the rest of the team.

To get up to speed with an enquiry that's been ongoing for some time was always difficult. Harriet knew she'd need to go back to the beginning, to look at early judgements and assumptions, to understand the decision-making process. She started with the Senior Investigating Officer's Policy

Document; this outlined the direction of the enquiry and detailed the decisions made based upon the available evidence at the time. She also studied the Forensic Strategy and Witness Strategies which had evolved from the Policy Document.

Initial nerves out of the way, Harriet started to do what she did best: pick out the salient points, focus on detail, identify anomalies and map the sequence of events. It did not take her long to identify aspects that might require further scrutiny.

Harriet was immediately struck by the similarities between the deceased men: all highly educated, with comparable lifestyles and interests. The lack of evidence to suggest they had known each other was frustrating, since they were all clearly linked by the identical way in which they had been laid out in death and the unusual post-mortem snake tattoos.

It was puzzling to Harriet too, that no definitive cause of death had yet been established. This went to the heart of the investigation. Was this a multiple murder enquiry or something else yet unexplained? Indeed, the investigation seemed to be making little progress to establish cause of death. A growing belief that poisoning might be responsible had not been actively pursued. It appeared that because it was initially thought the men may have died of natural causes, other possibilities had not been seriously considered until recently. This delay meant that the condition of the bodies had deteriorated to the point where it was unlikely that it would be possible to get definitive toxicology results. In a couple of cases, the bodies had been released back to the families and their funerals had taken place. It was far from an ideal situation.

As she was reading the available material on Professor Martin Grey, Harriet noticed Scenes of Crime had found a stone disc in a one of his trouser pockets. It was described as 'slightly larger than a two-pound coin'. It appeared to be solid and made of some sort of grey stone. Carved onto the face of the disc was the image of a sun or star containing sixteen points or beams. Harriet fetched the disc from the exhibit's store. Intrigued, she handled it through the evidence bag; it looked strangely familiar. She made the decision to request Scenes of Crime examine it more closely.

It was during the first few days of familiarisation that Harriet decided to test the water with DS Steve Smith. She did not yet feel sufficiently up to speed to contribute at the morning briefings, but she did have some questions.

Steve Smith was at his desk. Harriet placed a coffee on the desk. He looked up and smiled.

"Steve, sorry to interrupt your work, but do you mind if I ask a question about the investigation?"

"Of course, fire away."

"Do you know if anyone has looked at snake venom as a possible cause of death?"

"Why would they?"

"Well, because of the snake tattoos."

"Nope, don't think so, but let's face it, it's so improbable." Harriet wasn't sure, but she thought she detected a frown as he said this.

"Unusual, yes, but improbable? Surely it deserves to be ruled out?"

"It's rather fantastical, isn't it? But if you like I'll mention it to Nick. It may be that one of the other sergeants has been tasked with that enquiry."

Far from being put off by Steve Smith's dismissive response, Harriet decided to research the snake venom angle further. Nick kept his distance, remaining entrenched in his office at the far end of the room.

It was on the Thursday morning of Harriet's first week that Steve Smith first introduced her to her team. They looked a strange ad hoc bunch of tired looking detectives and young female admin staff.

As Harriet approached, she spotted Poppy Webster, the other party in the 'incident' with Nick. It was all she could do to keep on walking towards the group. Overcome with an intense desire to scream, to shout, to slap Poppy, it took all her self-control to stay in the room.

As Steve commenced the introductions, Harriet looked again at the young woman in front of her. She couldn't be more than twenty-two, a slip of a girl, with delicate features, a tiny waist, beautiful open face, and wavy shoulder length blonde hair. The situation was beyond awkward, but what she did now would define their working relationship. And, both she and Poppy were the focus of attention. Was it too early to tackle the elephant in the room? Poppy was visibly shaking as Harriet took her hand.

"Hello, it's good to meet you officially," she whispered in the girl's ear, smiling.

Wide-eyed, Poppy searched Harriet's face, and smiled back.

Next, Harriet was introduced to Detective Constable Mike Taylor, a skinny man in his late forties, with collar length ash blond hair, long side burns, wearing a dirty fawn Mac.

"Hello Mike, it's been a long time."

"It has indeed."

Harriet was introduced to the rest of the team, and chatted for a while, but she was distracted. She'd not seen Mike Taylor for many years; indeed, she'd quite successfully erased him from her memory, until today. She was surprised at just how uncomfortable he still made her feel.

With the introductions over, Harriet approached Poppy.

"Poppy, have you a minute?"

Poppy looked terrified.

"Grab your coat."

Harriet knew that their departure would create a stir. It was designed to.

They ordered coffee at a nearby café and found a table in the corner.

"I think we need to get the awkwardness out of the way." Harriet took a sip of coffee.

Poppy stared at the table. "I would really appreciate that. I've been in such a state," she whispered.

"I think we both need to move forward."

"But will they leave us alone? You know they deliberately put us together, so they could have a laugh at our expense." Poppy was tearful. She tugged at her hair.

It suddenly dawned on Harriet just how traumatised the girl before her was.

"I was working on DS Harvey's team. On the morning of your arrival, DS Steve Smith told me they had decided to churn some of the admin staff and that I was now to work with you. I watched him with his detective friends afterwards and they were laughing."

"Really? Interesting." Harriet folded her arms.

"Harriet, I never meant to hurt you, I bitterly regret what happened and I'm so embarrassed. I know it's no excuse, but I was very drunk. It was a lunchtime drink session that got out of hand. I'm so sorry, I've never done anything like this before. At the time I didn't think about what I was doing and now I'm the home-wrecker, the slag, the whore."

Harriet handed the weeping Poppy a tissue, before placing her hand on the young woman's shoulder.

"Please don't cry, we are where we are. I won't lie to you, I've been to hell and back. But, by the look of you, you have too. Look, we have a job to do. If we work together, it will take the wind out of the gossip's sails. They'll soon get bored and pick a new target. So, how about we go and get on with it?"

"Yes, let's do that."

Despite herself, Harriet had been moved by Poppy's

distress. Only time would tell if they would be able to work together.

Harriet had her first run-in with Mike Taylor in the first week. She had been waiting for him for over an hour to go through key statements.

"Mike, where have you been?"

"I got delayed." The absence of an explanation or an apology just served to add to Harriet's irritation.

"Clearly. Take a seat. Can you tell me if any of the families mention a stone disc about the size of a two-pound coin?"

Mike farcically shuffled through a pile of statements.

"I don't immediately recall. I don't think so."

Harriet took a deep breath. Mike Taylor was going to be a problem unless she took control. She had to remind herself that she was no longer the new probationer and he was no longer her tutor constable. No, time had moved on and now she was in charge.

"I'll see you here at eight thirty a.m. tomorrow, and please make sure you are fully conversant with the content of these statements."

Mike jumped to his feet. "You might be a fucking hotshot DS now, but you're not going to last long with your snotty attitude." He jabbed his right index finger in Harriet's face.

The incident room fell silent.

"Really? DC Taylor, how would you like to go back in uniform?" Harriet rose to her feet.

"You can't do that."

"Just try me."

Harriet hadn't meant to let him get under her skin so soon, but she still hadn't forgiven him for his treatment of her early in her career.

At lunchtime on Friday, Nick summoned Harriet to his office. It was inevitable that they would have to interact. Harriet was determined to be professional, but it did not stop her heart beating quicker than normal.

Nick was in a serious mood. "I want to run something past you before telling the rest of the team. Yesterday, I received a small hand-held tape recorder in the post. There was no note with it. It appears to contain the recording of the death of an unidentified male, at the hands of an unidentified female. I can only think it was sent because it relates to this investigation. But whose death it is, I've no idea. Have a listen, tell me what you think?"

"Is there a post mark on the package?"

"It's local, that's all I can say. Of course, it could be a hoax, but I'm hoping it's something we can follow up, that will move the investigation forward."

"Nick, can I quickly ask, has DS Steve Smith mentioned a conversation we had about snake venom?"

"Not that I recall."

"Okay, thanks. I'll listen to this and get back to you within the hour."

"Thank you. Was your conversation with Steve important?"

"No, it's okay, forget I mentioned it."

The Friday briefing took place in a meeting room next door to the incident room.

"Afternoon, everyone. I'm departing from our usual briefing and throwing the floor open to Detective Sergeant Harriet Lacey who, by the way, we are very lucky to have working with us. Whilst bringing herself up to speed, I thought it might be useful if she also reviewed the investigation. In addition, there has been a development which I will leave Harriet to explain. I understand Harriet has some queries for us," said Nick Lacey.

With churning stomach, Harriet got to her feet and forced a smile.

"Thank you, Sir. Afternoon all. My first question is to ask if any of you are aware of any tests being carried out to look for the presence of snake venom, both in relation to the bodies but also at the scenes of the deaths?"

"No, snake venom hasn't featured in the enquiry to date," said Nick. The team started to talk amongst themselves. Nick was forced to restore order and ask everyone to take their turn.

"Harriet, can you explain your rationale for asking?" said a curt Steve Smith. Harriet wondered what he was up to, particularly in view of their conversation earlier in the week.

"I just couldn't get the snake tattoos out of my mind. They are such a deliberate act, and I wondered whether they are perhaps a taunt? I kept asking myself why a snake and is it significant in some way? The tattoos are certainly one of only two common links we currently have between the deceased. As the initial post-mortems were unsuccessful in pin-pointing a cause of death, I wondered if it might be sensible to look for the presence of snake venom, if only to rule it out. Since some of the deceased are no longer available for scrutiny, and the remains of others have deteriorated, I wondered if Professor Grey's body might still be viable."

"Don't you think that's creating a huge amount of work, on a whim?" Steve Smith was staring directly at Harriet.

"What's the matter, Steve? You're usually the first to champion innovative lines of enquiry," said DS Harvey.

"I would just urge caution, that's all."

"Actually, I think Harriet may have something," said Nick, turning to the note-taker. "Note to myself to raise actions to request further investigation into the pathology of these deaths and to consider snake venom as a possible cause. Also, note to myself to request that Scenes of Crime go back to each of the scenes and take another look specifically for the presence of snake venom. Carry on, Harriet."

"I'm also interested to know if anyone has focussed on the way the dead men were laid out. Again, it appears a very deliberate act; is it religious or cultural, or is there another explanation? I couldn't find anything in the policy document to suggest this has been explored."

"That's an interesting point, and something that I confess I'd not considered. We will action this straight away," said Nick.

Harriet then proceeded to describe the package Nick had received the day before.

"What struck me were the similarities between the man's description of what was happening to him, and the symptoms of snake venom I'd researched."

"Harriet, are you sure you're not getting side-tracked? I mean, this could easily be a time-consuming distraction." Steve Smith was visibly flushed.

"I disagree Steve, it's intriguing. I think there may be merit in looking at this," said DS Harvey, interrupting for a second time.

"I think it's worth pursuing. I discovered that venom emitted from some snakes such as cobras, most sea snakes and mambas, contain toxins which attack the nervous system. This can lead to disturbed vision, which may include blurring; it can also cause paraesthesia, which to you and me, is 'pins and needles'. It seems that parts of the body begin to tingle and become numb, or 'fall asleep'. Some victims report having difficulty speaking and breathing. If the victim is not treated immediately, they may die from respiratory failure. Here, listen to part of the tape."

An elderly male could clearly be heard saying: "*There's a strange numbness coursing through my body, it started in my fingers and toes but it's quickly spreading to my legs and arms...*"

"It's feasible that this is one of our victims, but which one? I would suggest that we need to see if anyone recognises either of the voices," said Harriet.

Several heads nodded in agreement. Steve Smith however, looked far from happy.

"Well, I'm convinced. Let's pursue this and see where it

takes us. Thank you everyone," said Nick, drawing the briefing to a close.

As the team began to disperse, Harriet felt a hand on her shoulder. She turned to see DS Harvey standing next to her. He was a stocky man, Harriet guessed in his early forties, with an open face, kind eyes and bald head.

"Harriet, I just wanted to say I thought you did really well today. I know how hard it is to find your place in an established enquiry and I'm not the only one who was impressed. Don't mind Steve Smith, he's used to being 'top dog'. He's sulking, he'll get over it."

"Thanks Geoff, I really appreciated your support today." Geoff winked as he left the room.

Operation Chapel was officially back in business. Over the following week, the room buzzed with activity. When the results of the tests on Professor Grey came back positive for black mamba venom, the room was filled with renewed energy and Nick Lacey ordered further tests in respect of the remaining deceased.

Mike Taylor continued to press Harriet's buttons; there wasn't a day when they didn't have an altercation.

Harriet's fingers drummed the top of her desk. Twenty minutes later Mike sauntered in. His behaviour was becoming tiresome.

"Mike, where have you been?"

"Doing those bloody boring actions you tasked me with, you bitch," he muttered under his breath, but not low enough.

"What did you say?"

"I said I'd been doing those important actions you tasked me with, boss."

"That's pathetic, I heard you the first time. You are a pain in the arse."

He grinned back at her.

"You've been gone all day. Three actions, that's all you had; they should have been done and dusted by three o'clock at the latest. It's now gone six."

"Yeah, well, they took longer than anticipated."

"Yeah, well, the bitch has two more for you to do before you go off duty. And turn your mobile on," said Harriet as she put her coat on, picked up her bag and exited the room.

CHAPTER 7

It was a dark, damp late April evening. As she drove, Harriet's thoughts turned to her father, to his dementia, to how it was painfully tearing him away from his old self and from his family. Tears rolled down her cheeks. She wiped them away with the back of her hand.

A while later, she emerged from the supermarket with her groceries. As she rummaged for her keys, something struck her hard across the back of the head.

Momentarily disorientated, she fell to her knees and onto the shopping bags. But her training kicked in and she struggled to her feet just in time to see two shadowy figures running towards the alleyway. She gave chase. They were fast. Hurling herself forward she caught hold of the back of a black hooded sweatshirt; yanking the material as hard as she could, she downed the youth, rolled him onto his front and locked his arm up behind his back. But the other male had turned and was approaching, still clutching the piece of pipe he'd use to strike her. The blows fell hard and fast. Harriet winced but the onslaught was too much and she had to let go to protect herself. She managed to kick the pipe from her attacker's hand and an angry exchange of punches followed.

Breathless, she rasped, "What the hell do you think you are doing?" It had begun to rain.

No reply. She used all her strength to land an effective punch to her attacker's nose.

"Oh shit, shit, you've broken my nose you bitch, shit, shit, you weren't supposed to fight back." The youth clutched his face, blood flowing between his fingers.

"What the fuck did you just say?" Harriet scanned the unlit car park for someone to shout out to.

"You heard, bitch," said the other male. "We were told to give you a bit of a beating."

"Told by whom, moron?" Still there was no-one in sight. No reply.

Harriet recognised her situation: her attackers were both younger and fitter than her, and she was in a secluded area of the car park. She would not be able to last much longer; her head was pounding and her body sore. So, with as much effort as she could muster, she kicked out, managing to catch the youth in the black sweatshirt between the legs. As he fell to the ground screaming, she yanked her mobile from her jacket pocket and dialled 999.

A male operator answered. "Emergency, which service do you require: Fire, Police or Ambulance?"

"Police. I'm DS Harriet Lacey, an off-duty officer, currently at the top of Marlowe's car park in Western road. I'm being attacked by two males and need urgent..." The youth bleeding from the face had returned; he kicked the phone from her hand and punched her in the face. As she fell to the ground, she instinctively raised her arms above her head.

As Harriet lay face down, trying to shield herself, she thought she heard sirens in the distance. Were they getting closer? She prayed that they were coming to her aid. As abruptly as the beating had started, it stopped. Harriet was vaguely aware of the sound of fleeing footsteps which became fainter and fainter until she could no longer hear them. The sound of sirens on the other hand became deafening, then she was aware of flashing blue lights reflected in the puddle beside her head. Car doors slammed, there were footsteps, then a shout went up: she'd been found.

Cold and soaked through, Harriet was transported to hospital. The first person at her bedside was Nick.

He leaned forward and cupped her bruised and battered face in his hands. She did not pull away. God, she missed his touch and his smell. But she still hated him.

"I'm fine." But even she didn't think she sounded very convincing.

"Well, they most definitely picked the wrong person to mug." Nick perched on the edge of the bed.

"It wasn't a mugging, Nick."

"What do you mean?" Harriet could see the fear in his eyes.

"Something one of my attackers said."

"Harry, I don't like it. First the burglary, and now this. I really don't think you should be alone." He was ashen-faced.

"I'm fine."

"Have you seen yourself?"

She shook her head. He handed her make-up mirror over.

Slowly, she surveyed her face: a black and almost completely closed right eye, a grazed left cheek, and a swollen and cut lip.

"It could have been worse." She tried to wink. Nick began to laugh, and just for a moment, she laughed too.

"Harriet, you're being admitted. No, don't pull that face, it's just for tonight, just so they can keep an eye on you. I'll collect you tomorrow, I promise, and then you can rest at home, okay?"

"I suppose so." Suddenly she felt weary.

A couple of days later, Harriet was snoozing on the sofa in the garden room when she felt her mobile vibrate. It was Nick.

"Harriet, we have your attackers. The landlord of the 'Wobbly Duck' overheard them boasting about their exploits and called us. What a couple of muppets. Neither wore gloves, and their fingerprints are all over the pipe recovered from the scene. But, there is bad news too I'm afraid."

"Go on," she said sleepily.

"Well, DS Steve Smith volunteered to deal with the youths. It appears they told him that a mystery woman approached them outside the job centre. They describe her as pretty, but apparently could not, or would not, provide any further detail. They claimed to have been offered five hundred pounds to rough you up. In addition, when searched, they were found to have professional looking surveillance photos of you in their coat pockets. Steve Smith is convinced that this was a mugging and that the youths just made up their story. As neither have ever been in trouble with the police before, they were happy to admit assault and were issued with reprimands."

"Nick, slow down. I'm right here; you don't have to raise your voice."

"I really don't buy it was a mugging, but I seem to be the only one who's suspicious. Neither of their interviews lasted more than ten minutes. No way is that enough time to pick holes in their stories. And, no-one can explain how they came to have professional surveillance photos. In my opinion, the whole thing has just been brushed under the carpet. It's bloody outrageous; they assault a serving police officer and get a slap on the wrist. I've requested a full review of the Custody Officer's decision."

"Nick, take a breath. It's disappointing, but it's not by any means unusual and you know it. They caused bruising, they didn't break any of my limbs or cause any serious injuries. It happens in this job. And I would suggest you don't start a fight you can't win." The phone went dead.

Two hours later, her mobile vibrated again.

"Nick."

"Just wanted to tell you Superintendent Alec Brown finally called back."

"Did he? What did he say?"

"He was a bloody waste of space. Couldn't, or more likely wouldn't, tell me a bloody thing, but I put him in his place. I told him."

"There's no need to shout. What did you say to him? Please tell me you weren't too rude."

"I told him he was a complete imbecile, told him I'd go over his head and speak directly with Deputy Chief Constable Jack Peters."

"You didn't."

"Well, as it happens I was just about to pick up the phone when I got a call from Hillary Sellers."

"The Assistant Chief Constable? Really? That can't have been a coincidence, can it?"

"I've no bloody idea, but it didn't get me very far. Platitudes, just platitudes. She asked after you but when I pressed her about why you had been moved and who ordered it, she just said *'Sorry Nick, that's not something I'm party to.'* She would not be drawn further." Nick's emotional state was tiresome. Harriet wondered why he was so worked up.

"So, what now?"

"I don't bloody know. I think it's pointless to approach Jack Peters now, he's likely to be even more slippery. We will just have to be patient, it will come out at some juncture, I've no doubt."

Harriet was relieved when the conversation came to an end. Contact with Nick was becoming increasingly demanding; there was something different about him.

CHAPTER 8

It was a week and a half before Harriet was well enough to return to work. Still stiff from the beating, the bruises on her face were conspicuous.

"Harriet, it's so good to see you." Poppy handed her a coffee and chocolate muffin.

Harriet scrutinised her face; she still wasn't sure how she felt about Poppy, but she did appear genuinely pleased to see her.

"Thank you, it's good to be back. Cake and coffee, you're spoiling me."

Poppy grinned. She pulled up a chair. "Okay, you should know that whilst you were away most of the activity has involved liaising with the other police forces and reinterviewing family members. Also, further tests have been conducted on the deceased or in some cases their blood and tissue samples. I think we may learn more about this at the briefing later. Let's hope there's been a breakthrough. Also, Mike has been looking at the way the bodies were laid out post-death. I'll get him to talk you through it."

A couple of hours later Nick emerged from his office and asked everyone to gather round.

"I'll be quick, but I just wanted you to hear what DS Paul Jones from Scenes of Crime has just told me. He's just finished reading the pathologist's reports and we have the break-through we'd been praying for. Sergeant Lacey's hunch was right. Each of the deceased tested positive for the presence of snake venom, but it's in such concentrations that it could not have been a snake bite, rather it had to have been administered. Tests are continuing with a view to discovering how the venom got into the men's systems, but there is no doubt in Paul's mind that it was responsible for these men's deaths."

Announcement over, Mike sidled up to Harriet's desk. "Well, that was a bit of a bombshell."

Harriet didn't feel like a fight, she hoped Mike would give her a break.

"Yes, grab a chair."

"I've looked at current funeral customs for the most common religions including Christianity, Judaism, Hinduism, Islam, Buddhism, and Sikhism, none seem to fit. I've also looked at some of the most common cults, such as Scientology, the Moonies, the Order of the Solar Temple, and Children of God. Again, no good fits. So, I began to think that perhaps the practice had its roots in the past." Mike consulted his notes.

"Good thinking, have you got anywhere with that?"

"Well, it's early days, but I think I might be making progress. I have a meeting coming up with a BBC researcher friend who has suggested that we look at practice in the ancient world. She's going to help me follow it up."

"That's great, thank you Mike, good work."

The following day, Harriet was poring over further statements when the phone broke her concentration. She picked up the receiver.

"Harriet Lacey."

"Good morning Harriet, Paul Jones here, how the devil are you?" Harriet loved his broad Welsh accent.

"Much improved, Paul, and thank you for the beautiful flowers."

Harriet liked Paul Jones, a short and round, middle-aged Welsh man, with a crop of unruly auburn hair. He was partial to wearing brightly coloured waistcoats, corduroy trousers and wellington boots. Although slightly eccentric, he was extremely competent at his job.

"Oh, it was the least we could do for our favourite sergeant; Harriet, about the results of the swabs taken from your burglary, I think you might find them curious."

'Curious' was an interesting choice of words, thought Harriet as her breathing quickened.

"Well, it seems that the tool used to prise open the garden door left a residue behind. I have to say that it stumped us, until, that is, one of our officers recognised the chemical structure from Professor Martin Grey's post-mortem report."

Harriet shuddered.

"Are you still with me?" Paul sounded excited.

Harriet closed her eyes. "Yes."

"Believe it or not, it was snake venom."

"Are you sure?"

"Oh yes, but it's not just snake venom, it's black mamba," said Paul eagerly.

Something sinister was going on. Her stomach churned.

"Are you absolutely a hundred percent sure?"

"Oh yes, there's no doubt whatsoever, I'll send you the report."

"Thank you, and I appreciate the heads-up, but please don't mention this to anyone else, not just yet."

"You're sure?"

"Yes, sure, and thank you again, Paul."

Harriet felt every muscle in her body tighten. Reluctant to tell Nick about the latest development, she pondered her situation. She had to trust someone; she couldn't do this on her own. Grudgingly, she concluded that someone was going to have to be Mike Taylor. She needed his contacts and experience to track down her assailants. She needed to find out more about the mysterious woman. Despite their differences, Mike was a good detective; she had little choice, anyway, there was no-one else to ask.

CHAPTER 9

While Harriet waited for Mike Taylor to arrive in the incident room, she thought about how his attitude had softened since the assault on her. Shortly after nine, he appeared at his desk.

"I don't know what you've got on today, but I did wonder if you might be able to help me with an enquiry." Harriet handed him a coffee.

"Yes sure, I'm meeting with my BBC friend first thing, how about eleven?"

"Eleven's fine."

"What do I need to prepare, my lady?" Mike was grinning. Harriet appreciated his cheek and smiled back.

"Nothing, I will brief you on the way."

Harriet drove, mainly because she knew it annoyed Mike and although she wanted him on her side, any change to their normal routine would make him suspicious. Leaving their unmarked police vehicle in a side street, they walked a quarter of a mile to a stylish coffee shop where Harriet bought two coffees. They sat in silence for a few minutes.

"Mike, I'm taking a huge risk in speaking to you, a huge risk trusting you, but right now, I don't have anyone else." Harriet braced herself for some sarcastic comment, but he remained silent.

"There is no easy way to say this but what I'm going to tell you is confidential, is that understood?"

Mike simply nodded.

"I'm pretty sure there's been an organised attempt to warn me off Operation Chapel."

"Really?" He sounded genuinely surprised.

"I don't know if you heard about the burglary at my house recently."

"Yeah, fucking bad luck that."

"It's more than that, Mike. Yesterday, I learned from DS Paul Jones that Scenes of Crime found traces of snake venom on the entry point. They think it's from the tool used to jemmy-open the French doors. But, it wasn't just any old snake venom, it was black mamba."

"Fuck," said Mike, wide-eyed.

"Then, when I was attacked in the car park, one of my attackers taunted me by saying a mystery woman paid them to assault me. I never got to ask any more and it appears the investigating officer failed to cover it in interview."

"How'd you know that?" Mike was sitting on the edge of his chair.

"Because I pulled a favour and managed to get a copy of the file. I had the interview tapes transcribed and let's just say they were bloody disappointing."

"Didn't Steve Smith personally lead the investigation?"

"Yes, and on the surface it's puzzling that such an experienced detective missed such an obvious line of ques-tioning."

"Are you saying you think Smith deliberately sabotaged the interview?"

"I'm not sure what to think, but I'm suspicious."

Mike frowned.

"I hope you don't think I'm being paranoid, Mike, but I'm wondering if there is a link between the snake venom at my house, the snake venom used to kill our victims, and the mystery woman."

"I'd say it's possible. So, I'm guessing that you want me to track down your attackers to see if I can find out more about the mystery woman, but you want this done under the radar, right?"

"Yes, please."

"You can trust me, you know." He was looking directly at her, and in that instant she knew she could.

They finished their coffee and returned to the incident room, where the daily briefing was about to start. Mike and Harriet stood at the back. Harriet thought Nick looked distracted, he was unshaven and seemed more interested in his phone than the briefing.

"Morning everyone, we have a lot to get through."

It was soon time for Harriet's team to provide their update. Harriet got to her feet.

"We've been concentrating on the statements of the victims' family members, we still have a few to look at but what we've found so far is interesting. Commonality between at least four of the victims, in terms of a fear of snakes and possession of a stone disc identical to that found in Professor

Grey's pocket. I'll read you some extracts." Harriet picked up her note book and read aloud.

'My father had a lifelong revulsion of snakes, to us it seemed irrational. He never did explain why. He also kept what he called his 'good luck charm' with him, he even slept with it under his pillow. He said it was his protection from the serpents... The charm was a round smooth piece of stone slightly larger than a two-pound coin. On one side it was smooth, on the other engraved with what looked like a sun with lots of pointed beams.'

'Dad loathed snakes, when we were little and at the Zoo he would point-blank refuse to accompany us to the reptile house. He never budged from this position, never. Dad also had this annoying habit of playing with a small smooth stone token, in and out of his fingers, it drove me mad.'

'My old Dad used to play with a stone disc, twisting it in and out of his fingers, over and over, a bit like worry beads. He hated snakes, if they ever came on the TV he would immediately scream for the controls and change the channel.'

"Good work; keep going with this and update us at the next briefing, will you? Just out of interest, how many of the stone discs have been recovered so far?" Nick walked across to Harriet.

"Four." Harriet was sure she could smell alcohol on his breath.

"Okay, well, keep going with this line of enquiry please. Now, how have you got on with your enquiries, Mike? Is there anything significant about the way the bodies were laid out?"

"Well, Sir, I think I might have found that it was common

practice historically, several cultures laid out their dead in a similar way; in other words a coin or other valuable item was put in the mouth or between the lips to enable the deceased to move to the afterlife, rather than remain in limbo."

"But there were no valuables left with our victims."

"Apparently not, unless you include the possibility that the stone discs had value."

"I might be able to add to this debate," said DS Paul Jones, who had entered the room.

"Go ahead, Paul." Nick waved Paul to the front of the room.

"A few weeks ago, DS Lacey requested Scenes of Crime take a closer look at the stone disc found in Professor Grey's pocket. To our utter surprise, we discovered that it's not actually made of stone at all, but rather, it's a type of cement. Further tests have revealed that it's archaic, certainly pre-Roman, but what's even more fascinating is that the cement is an outer layer. It was used to encase a gold coin." A stir went around the briefing room.

"The coin itself weighs 8.59 grams and has a diameter of 18.5 mm. On one side is the depiction of a man with curly hair and beard, on the other a naked youth on horseback. I've taken the liberty of contacting the British Museum who have kindly agreed to study it further and give their expert view. It could take a week or two."

"Blimey, well as soon as you hear back, please let me know the result." Nick made a note in his policy document. Paul Jones nodded.

As the discussion in the room continued, Harriet glanced

across at Steve Smith. He seemed uncharacteristically silent but was making copious notes.

"Shall I move on?" asked Paul Jones.

"Yes, what else do you have for us?" said Nick. Harriet surveyed the room; all eyes were on Paul Jones, or 'Jonesy' as he was affectionately known.

"We've been looking at the venom and have discovered that just a couple of drops of black mamba venom can kill a human. The venom contains neurotoxins and is fast acting, shutting down the nervous system, it paralyses the victim. Without anti-venom, death is a hundred percent certain." Excited chatter filled the room.

"Sorry to interrupt again, Paul, but I want it recorded that actions are raised for enquiries to be carried out into possible sources of black mamba venom. Can it be purchased on the web? Is it feasible it was imported? Or farmed? Thanks, carry on," said Nick.

"I just want to talk about the scenes you asked us to re-examine. We can confirm that they were cleaned down. There were no fingerprints or DNA on key surfaces, except that is at Professor Martin Grey's house. And, whilst there was evidence of a clean up there, we did find several clear fingerprints at the points of entry and egress and around the body. My early guess is that these were made after the initial wipe down, as we didn't find any of the victim's prints in the same area. They are good quality prints and we've already run them through the National Fingerprint Database, but with no hits, so they remain outstanding."

Nick turned to the note-taker. "Note to myself: create a policy decision requesting fingerprinting of persons of interest in this case. I'll do this later. Paul, is there anything else that might help us with the fingerprints to narrow it down?"

"Well, there's good news and bad news. Although we didn't manage to get any full DNA profiles, other than from the victims, because of the sterile scenes. At Professor Grey's, it was clear someone touched some of the surfaces, for we did find low copy DNA. There's a chance we may get lucky and get a profile, but it's going to take some time. As you know with low copy DNA it isn't as accurate as when you have a full profile, but it could help us to narrow down the field of suspects."

"How long will that take? Make sure you fast-track it." Nick had got to his feet.

"Yeah, it's fast-tracked but it could still take two weeks, as it's only a small sample."

CHAPTER 10

It was a beautifully sunny Saturday morning when Harriet rang the doorbell at number 26 Hawthorn Avenue. Her mother, Jane, opened the door and greeted her warmly, hugging her long and hard. Harriet thought her mother looked drawn and tired, her tall slender frame moved more stiffly than she remembered. Harriet walked down the light airy hall and turned left into the lounge. Her father was seated with his back to her in his favourite brown leather chair. Had he sensed her? For, as she entered the room, he stood up and turned, his face lighting up. He moved slowly towards her outstretched arms and hugged her tight.

"You, I thought, lovely see fit you?"

Harriet had become accustomed to interpreting her father's jumbled words.

"Lovely to see you too, Dad. Yes, I'm well, thank you." She held him close.

Harriet looked at her father; at 6 ft 2, George Rayfield was a large-framed man, but his illness had taken its toll; he looked frail, and was carrying little weight. His hair, almost white, stuck out from beneath a dark blue knitted hat and he was sporting a beard.

Jane appeared with a tray of coffee and a plate of homemade shortbread biscuits. They moved to the sofa and

73

George sat between his wife and his daughter. Harriet joked that he was a rose between two thorns. Although he did not seem to understand their chatter, he looked mightily happy to be there. Harriet held her father's hand tight.

After coffee, Harriet and George wandered around the garden arm in arm, inspecting the plants, the pond, the green house and the vegetable plot. Leaving her father sitting in the sunshine, she went to find her mother.

"So, Dad's grown a beard."

"Yes, the Warfarin thins the blood. Your Dad was finding it increasingly difficult to shave and after several nasty nicks to his face that bled and bled, I simply removed his razor from the bathroom. Funny thing is he doesn't seem to have noticed."

"What about his woolly hat?"

"Your Dad's become increasingly obsessed with certain items of clothing, the latest being the woolly hat. His jumpers are all now heavily patched and holey. I have to grab them when I can, mend them, wash them and return them without him noticing, otherwise he becomes distressed."

"But he always used to be so fastidious, always clean shaven; always in a shirt and tie and a sports jacket or smart jumper."

"Yes, before he became unwell."

George could no longer read, no longer follow the television, no longer hold a conversation, but, he loved to leaf through old photograph albums. In one of the albums, Harriet came across a smiling photo of him. He was standing in what looked like an archaeological site wearing khaki shorts, a white shirt with the sleeves rolled up and a floppy sun hat. Behind him she could see a stone doorway; at its centre point there was a carving that caught Harriet's eye. It looked like a sun, it had sixteen points or beams to it. Harriet asked her mother about the photo.

"I think it was about twenty-five years ago in Greece, at a royal palace, but I can't remember exactly where."

"May I borrow it?"

"Of course, borrow the album if you like."

When Harriet left, she hugged and kissed her father and said her goodbyes. As she reached her car, he called from the doorstep.

"Harry, beware of the serpents, the sun is the path to enlightenment."

Stunned, Harriet turned and went back to the house, but her father was listless and unable to make himself understood.

Gone was the laid back, happy and optimistic man who for twenty years had been Professor of Ancient History and Classical Archaeology at Sheffield University. A true gentleman and scholar. Loved by his students and colleagues. To watch the man who had lived his life by the written and spoken word, the man Harriet admired above all others, slip away was agonising.

Her mother enveloped her in her arms.

"Harry, why don't you take some books from your Dad's library and that bundle of his old handwritten note books?"

That evening Harriet began to look through her father's note books. In one of them she came across a pencil drawing of the sun symbol she'd seen in the photo earlier. It struck her that it was remarkably like the symbols on the stone discs from Operation Chapel. Her father had scribbled:

Today, on the eastern edge of the main site, we discovered a hoard of around fifty rounded stone tokens, stashed in the remains of a large villa. Smooth on one side, carved with what looks like a sixteen-point sun on the other. This symbol occurs on many of the palace doorways, as well as the main archway to the amphitheatre.

It was then that Harriet remembered a letter her father had sent her when she'd been about thirteen. He'd been working abroad and was keen to share his experiences with her. She tried to think where she'd stored it. As a child, she'd often kept special correspondence in an old shoe box. But where had she put it? Eventually she found it in an old wardrobe in the attic. The letter was still in its original envelope.

During our excavations, we've found an incomplete stone tablet, it hints at a war between the women in King Philip's life, following his assassination. The reason for the conflict appears to centre on the fate of his children. The translation is still being worked on, but the closest I can get to it is that the fight was between the 'Guardians' and the 'Serpents'·

You know, I've always been fascinated as to what happened to Philip's offspring after he died· The historian Justin refers to the existence of several brothers to Alexander, born to Philip's mistresses – some believe Alexander executed his step-brothers, but they may have survived and there were undoubtedly other children, half-sisters for example, who were unlikely to have been considered a threat to the throne· But, there are also references to certain females in the family being trained as warriors, for example, his first wife Audata, and their daughter Cynane·

You know, I admire King Philip· It's often forgotten that he was the only King ever to unite the Greek world· History, however, has chosen to concentrate on his son Alexander, or Alexander the Great as he came to be known, following his invasion of Persia· But it was Philip who made that possible, who spent years building a professional army, making strategic alliances and treaties across the Greek world· What he achieved is truly remarkable·

I sometimes wonder what he was really like as a man· There are hints in the history books, but many Greek historians at the time did not like him, referring to him as a 'barbarian', or accusing him of insatiable ambition, or of breaking treaties· There were others *who described him as charming, charismatic, astute politically, of displaying unusual courage· But conversely, he's also been labelled as overly extravagant, a man who drank too much and who was quick to temper· There are also tantalising references to injuries he incurred, such as a leg wound, serious enough to cause him to limp and the suggestion that an arrow blinded him in the right eye· You know, I suspect he was a bit of all of the above, a lovable rogue!*

Putting the letter to one side, Harriet wondered if it was feasible that events that occurred so long ago could really have a bearing today. It seemed crazy. Could the stone discs from Operation Chapel really be linked to those found by her father twenty-five years before? And what had happened to these? And what about his words to her? *"Harry, beware of the serpents, the sun is the path to enlightenment."* Was this significant? Was it linked to the reference in his letter to a possible battle between the Guardians and the Serpents? Or were they just the demented ramblings of a tortured mind? Too tired to ponder this further, Harriet turned in for the night.

CHAPTER 11

Rain lashed the garden doors. Harriet peered at the stormy scene outside, the wet trees bending in the breeze. It was in stark contrast to her father's sunny garden the day before. Still in her dressing gown and nursing a mug of coffee, she looked at the clock at the far end of the kitchen; in a few hours Ben and Amelia would arrive for Sunday lunch. She turned to put the oven on and was about to go for a shower when her mobile burst into life. It was Derek Wynn.

"Hello Harriet, sorry to ring you on a Sunday, but I need to have a word. I was hoping to speak to Nick at the same time, but I'm having difficulty tracking him down."

"Sorry, I don't know where he is. What is it that you want?"

"Well, as I was jogging this morning I spotted a red-faced Alec Brown emerge from some foliage onto the path in front of me. He was waving me over. He looked rather like an overweight and overdressed twitcher."

"Oh, stop, please," said Harriet, laughing. "Whatever did he want?"

"To tell me he was in trouble, trouble of his own making. It's a long story but essentially he got himself involved with a group of high-profile individuals, and for years, he's run around doing their bidding in return for generous payment. At first it was little favours, no questions asked, but as time went on, the requests became more and more involved. It wasn't long before he realised that he'd crossed the line."

"The corrupt bastard, but how is this relevant?"

"Well, I'm about to get onto that. It would seem he's grown a conscience. When the decision was made to move you from Operation Eagle to Chapel, he was given the job of delivering the news."

"Yes, I remember the enthusiasm with which he did that," said Harriet, frowning.

"Quite, but when Nick confronted him, he found himself showing off and went off script. For some reason, and he still doesn't know why, he blurted out that the move was for your own safety. Understandably, Nick was alarmed, and demanded answers."

"I knew Nick was holding something back from me."

"Really? Anyway, now Alec had a problem. When he confessed his mistake to his boss, he was berated, but then his boss decided Alec's slip presented an opportunity."

"An opportunity for what?"

"To warn you off, discourage you."

"Bloody hell, what else did he say?"

"That they have placed someone on Operation Chapel, and this person is really impressing the hierarchy."

"Do we know who this is?"

"No, Brown refused to say. But Brown believes that you are now truly in danger, particularly if you continue to progress Chapel."

"Seriously?"

"Yes, you sound as sceptical as I was, but he anticipated this. He's no fool, so he recorded part of a conversation with his boss. Here. Listen."

A male voice could clearly be heard saying *"Alec, this better be good."*

Then Brown: *"Sir, I am sorry to bother you, but 'our friend' reports Harriet is pursuing a line of enquiry into the possibility that snake venom is involved in the Chapel deaths."*

Then the other male: *"Shit, shit, shit."*

And Brown: *"'Our friend' doesn't think it will be too long before she makes the link between Eagle and Chapel."*

"There's a link?" Harriet asked.

"It would appear so, the recording ends with the other man saying:

"Well, we can't have that, so we'll have to make sure that she doesn't make that link, won't we? What is it about that woman, why can't she just keep a low profile, for fuck's sake?"

"That's a bit rude. Do you know who that is?"

"I think I might, but I really don't want to say anything quite yet, if that's okay? I've strongly advised Alec to make a copy of the recording, and place it somewhere safe. I've also suggested that he disappears for a bit, perhaps takes some leave. In the meantime, I will try to track Nick down; apart from anything, we need to discuss what we are going to do about Brown."

"That sounds sensible."

"Now, as far as you're concerned, I think we need to take sensible precautions. Later this afternoon, technical support will call by; I've asked them to review your security. At the very least we need a panic alarm, and cameras on all entry and exit points. Can you dig out the IMEI number on your mobile for them? Also, I need you to make a note of Incident 67 and today's date. It's restricted, it details these measures and gives instructions to the control room, should you call in."

"I really appreciate that, thank you, Sir."

CHAPTER 12

The following afternoon Harriet arranged to meet Mike for a second time at the coffee shop. Keen to find out if he had located her assailants, she got there early.

"How did you get on? Did you manage to track my attackers down?"

"I did. They met the mystery woman in the park, just off Highland Avenue, on the morning of the attack. She gave them verbal instructions."

"What about the surveillance photos?"

"Handed out to them at the same time. They had no knowledge of where these came from, or indeed how long you'd been subject to surveillance. Your attackers were amateurs, but they did provide a half decent description. They described the woman as exceptionally confident, mid- to late-twenties, with long dark hair tied in a loose pony tail, immaculately made up, with stunning green eyes. What is interesting, however, is that one of the guys caught a glimpse of a tattoo on the inside of her left wrist."

"A tattoo of what?"

"A snake."

"Really? Really? I didn't expect that."

"I know. They apparently communicated via a pay-as-you go mobile. It's no longer live. When she left the meeting, they saw her drive away in a white Range Rover. No index though," said Mike.

He leaned forward and placed his hand on Harriet's arm. "There is one other thing: apparently before she left, the mystery woman joked with them that if you didn't get the message soon, your immediate family would have to be the next target."

Harriet could not catch her breath.

"You're not on your own, I'm here." Mike kept his hand on Harriet's arm.

"Listen, you are a remarkable officer, with a reputation for being a bit of a terrier. This is not going to beat you, okay?"

Harriet nodded and took hold of Mike's hand.

"I think there are a couple of things we should do straight away. Firstly, move your children out of harm's way. The less people who know the better. Secondly, speak to Nick; he has a right to know what's been going on, you need to bring him up to speed. Despite your personal difficulties, he is Ben and Amelia's father and Senior Investigating Officer on Chapel."

Harriet could only manage another nod, but she was more grateful to Mike than she could ever say.

CHAPTER 13

Harriet could not sleep. Each time she closed her eyes shapes and silhouettes of serpents appeared. In the end, she sat in the kitchen drinking tea until the clock chimed 7 a.m.

"You sound stressed," said Annie as soon as she heard Harriet's voice.

"I'm in a bit of a spot. Is there any chance you could have Ben and Amelia for a bit?"

"I would love to have them, it would be an absolute pleasure."

"Thank you, Annie. I'm sorry though, I can't tell you what's going on, save to say the kids mustn't contact any of their friends or family for a while. It's important that they vanish. I'll text you the details later."

"Don't worry my dear. I'll take good care of them. Now, stay safe and don't do anything risky."

"Thank you so much. I will, I promise, and please be on your guard."

"Not a problem, speak soon."

Later, between meetings, Harriet made another call.

"Good Morning, St Bartholomew's School, how can I help?" said one of the school secretaries.

"Morning, it's Harriet Lacey, Ben and Amelia's Mum. Could I possibly have a quick word with the Headteacher, Mr Jones? It's rather important."

"Oh, I'm sorry, love." Harriet winced, but decided to let it go. "He's covering the Deputy Head's history class; would you like to ring back about twelve thirty?"

"Look, I wouldn't ask if it wasn't important."

"Sorry, love, he's teaching; please ring back later."

Before Harriet could respond, the call terminated. Harriet redialled.

"Good Morning, St Bartholomew's School, how can I help?"

"It's Detective Sergeant Harriet Lacey again," she said, resorting to using her job title. She didn't have time to mess around. "I have to speak to Mr Jones, it concerns the safety of students. It's imperative that I have a conversation with him now, this is a safeguarding matter."

The silence at the other end of the phone seemed interminable.

"Look, do I have to come to the school and drag him out of the classroom myself?" shouted Harriet, immediately regretting losing her cool.

Some minutes later a breathless Mr Jones was on the other end of the phone.

"Good morning Mrs Lacey, what can I do for you?"

"I need your help. A serious situation has arisen; Ben and Amelia are in danger. To elaborate would also place you in danger."

"Oh gosh, well of course, just hang on a second while I close my office door." There was a pause. "So, what is it that you would like me to do, Mrs Lacey?"

"In the next ten minutes, a man called Mike Taylor, a colleague of mine, will arrive at the school with train tickets for Ben and Amelia, a change of clothes for both children and a couple of pay-as-you-go mobiles. Can I ask that you organise somewhere for them to change? Then could you take them to the station, and put them on the correct train?"

"Yes, I can do that."

"I'm most grateful. Would you also mind asking Ben to call me en route, on my work mobile?"

"Yes, I can do that too."

"I don't know how to thank you. I promise I will return them to school as soon as possible. There is just one more thing. I can't emphasise enough how important it is that no-one else knows about this."

"I understand."

"If anyone does ask about the children, please don't give anything away. They will likely be most persuasive, no doubt telling you it's an emergency, but don't be fooled."

"Mrs Lacey, don't worry, leave it with me."

"Thank you so much."

About an hour later, Harriet's mobile rang.

"Mum? It's Ben."

"Ben, thank you for calling, are you both okay?"

"Yes, we're fine, but what's going on, Mum?"

"That's a difficult one, Ben, just listen carefully."

"No problem." His reply was uncharacteristically mature.

"Dad and I love you both so much, but something has happened at work and as a result, we need to make sure you are both safe. There are some unscrupulous people who may try to get to you to hurt Dad and me. So, we need to make sure you are safely out of the way. Try to look at it as a bit of an adventure for a few days."

"It's okay Mum, we are cool with it, but we would kind of like to know where we are going."

"To Sheffield. At the station, you will be met by a very dear friend of mine, Annie. She was a student of Granddad Rayfield's. She's going to look after you for a few days on her smallholding. She's great fun, a real character."

"That sounds alright, and far better than being at school."

"Ben, it's really important that both you and Amelia only use the new phones you've been given. And, don't be tempted to contact any of your friends, not yet anyway, nor your grandparents. We don't accidentally want to put them in danger too. The best thing for everyone is if you just disappear for a while."

"Yes, I understand, but promise me that you are both okay?"

"We are and feel so much better for knowing you are safe."

"Mum, are we a dysfunctional family?"

"What do you mean?"

"Oh, it's just that lately we are pretty much living with Dad's parents full-time. You and Dad can't bear the sight of each other. Granddad Rayfield has taken to wandering around mumbling about snakes and Queens and 'trouble' and now issues at work mean we are being sent away."

"Well, if you say it like that, I suppose we are in a bit of a pickle."

"Pickle, Mum? Really? I'm fifteen!"

"Okay, then things, yes, things are a bit shit."

Ben laughed.

"Changing the subject, was Mr Jones okay?" Harriet asked.

"He was actually very nice, bought us sandwiches and drinks for the journey. I think he enjoyed the intrigue."

It was Harriet who was laughing now. "I love you Ben Lacey, give my love to Amelia and I'll speak to you later."

"I will, and love you too, Mum."

CHAPTER 14

Nick was not in his office, but his phone was ringing. She picked it up.

"SIO's office, Harriet Lacey speaking, how can I help?"

"Harriet, it's Derek Wynn. Is Nick there by any chance? I still haven't managed to speak to him."

"He isn't, but I'm about to track him down. Why don't you come across?"

Just as Harriet dialled her mother-in-law's number, a rather dishevelled and unshaven Nick walked in.

"You look awful," said Harriet, replacing the handset. "Is everything alright?"

"Everything's fine. I just overslept that's all, no big deal." Nick sounded irritable.

"Derek Wynn is on his way, he's been trying to get hold of you for a few days."

Wynn arrived, and Harriet left the two men to talk.

When she was summoned back, Nick was shaking his head.

"We need to talk, make some decisions." Harriet could see the fear in his eyes.

"I'd like Mike Taylor to join us," she said.

"Yeah sure, ask him in. Before I forget, Mr Jones from the school called for you."

"How long ago?"

"Oh, about an hour I think," he said glancing at his watch. "Is it important?"

"It might be."

"Well, I'm sorry, I didn't know." He pulled a face.

"No, it's okay. I've had to arrange for the kids to stay with Annie, you know my friend from Sheffield?" Nick nodded.

Anticipating his next question, Harriet continued. "Mike discovered they might be in danger. It seems I was assaulted in an attempt to dissuade me from continuing to work on Operation Chapel. When this failed, it was thought that I might toe the line if my family were threatened."

"Is this for real?" Nick got to his feet looking from Harriet to Derek.

"It would appear so," said Derek.

"Bloody hell. You are sure they're safe?"

"Yes, sure."

"I need to make a quick call to the school. I won't be a minute," said Harriet. Derek went in search of Mike.

"Mr Jones? It's Harriet Lacey; sorry for the delay in getting back to you. I've put you on speaker phone, it's perfectly safe to speak."

"Mrs Lacey, about half an hour after I returned from the train station, I received a charming visitor at school, your cousin Tracey Webb. She informed me that due to a family emergency you had asked her to collect the children. I told her that Ben was in an exam and, family emergency or not, could not be disturbed, and Amelia was on a school trip. She thanked me and left."

"Well done, thank you. You know, I do have a cousin called Tracey Webb. What did she look like?"

"Tall, mid- to late-twenties, slender, dark hair tied in a pony tail, smartly dressed, in a grey trouser suit, striking."

"You were right to be suspicious; my cousin is blonde, short, thick-set and aged about fifty now I think. I can't thank you enough, you know it's possible she may try again."

"And I will be ready, Mrs Lacey, please don't worry."

Harriet turned to the others. Derek had returned with Mike.

"Bloody good job, Harriet." Nick took a swig from a bottle of water, or at least it looked like water. "I bloody knew it. I knew it. Bloody Steve Smith," screamed Nick.

"What?" Nick's sudden change of subject alarmed Harriet.

"I knew I was right, that it was no mugging. Steve Smith has some explaining to do. He's supposed to be a bloody experienced detective." Nick paced up and down.

"Sir, would it be helpful if Mr Wynn and I reviewed the assault?" said Mike. Derek put a calming hand on Nick's shoulder.

"Thank you, yes. Good idea."

"Nick, there's something else." Harriet leant against the wall wondering how Nick would react to her next revelation.

"DS Paul Jones has discovered that the tool used to jemmy

the French doors at our house left traces of snake venom behind. Black mamba venom, to be exact."

"Oh my god. What the hell is going on?" Nick jumped to his feet.

"I'd say that the most likely explanation is there's an organised attempt by a person or persons unknown to interfere with this investigation," said Derek.

"Nick, please don't take this the wrong way, but in my opinion this enquiry needs to be cranked up a level. We need to push on, to seize the advantage. To be honest the investigation is too slow, it lacks both focus and impetus. Basic enquiries are taking too long to accomplish." Harriet placed her hands on her hips.

"Like what?" Nick sounded defensive.

"Well for starters, it's been weeks since it was agreed that the deceased family and friends should be canvassed to see if anyone recognised either of the voices on the tape sent in the post. These enquiries are still outstanding." No-one said anything.

"You know what, I'm going to progress this right now," said Harriet, slamming both hands down on Nick's desk. "I suggest you stay here and discuss what you're going to do about Alec Brown." She strode out of the office and shouted across to Poppy. "Are you free?"

Poppy nodded.

"Good, get your coat, we're going for a drive."

As she drove, she wondered if she had overstepped the mark in Nick's office. She'd certainly let her frustration spill over. But she could not shake a strong sense of foreboding. Nick seemed distracted and out of sorts, just when they needed a strong leader. If she were honest, he wasn't the right person to head up the enquiry.

Two hours later, Harriet and Poppy were driving back from their enquiry.

"I can't believe how quickly Professor Grey's housekeeper Mrs Briggs recognised his voice," said a smiling Harriet. But she also could not forget the horror on the face of Mrs Briggs as she listened to the tape. Although Professor Grey had been her employer, he'd also been her dear friend.

Poppy turned onto the dual carriageway. There were few cars on the road. She moved into the nearside lane and drove at a steady speed. A fast-moving grey truck appeared alongside. It slowed and Harriet noticed the driver peering in at them.

Poppy laughed. "I think that idiot wants to race."

The truck sped off, but as Poppy turned the corner, it was once again in sight. As they approached, it abruptly veered into their path and screeched to a halt, side on. There was no escaping it, no time to brake. The sound of crunching metal was deafening. The force of the impact slammed their car into the kerb, before it somersaulted off the carriageway into a tree.

Harriet felt her body fly forwards; her seatbelt locked, she was jolted back so violently that she did not feel the impact with the windscreen.

When she regained consciousness, she felt strange, woolly; she tried to take in her surroundings but her vision was blurred. She had begun to shake. The acrid odour of overheated electrics and diesel permeated the car. Glancing to her right, she saw the driver's door had crumpled inwards, partially enveloping Poppy.

Poppy's blonde hair was wet with perspiration. She was unresponsive. Harriet scrabbled around for her phone, eventually finding it in the footwell. She dialled 999. Then she tried to find a pulse. None was detectable in Poppy's left wrist, but maybe a faint one in her neck? She couldn't be sure.

Stroking Poppy's left cheek, she tried to assess the extent of her injuries. It was impossible to move her; the right side of her body was engulfed by the door. Pale and clammy to the touch, her breathing was almost undetectable.

"Hold on, Poppy, please hold on, help is on its way," said Harriet. "It's going to be okay, please stay with me. Come on, fight, please Poppy!"

Several witnesses had stopped and were crossing the carriageway. Compelled to do something more, Harriet carefully exited the car; she felt weak and unsteady on her feet. Using the car to support her, she carefully made her way round to the driver's side, to a scene of destruction. The tree was tight against the door. There was no space to manoeuvre. In that instance she knew the situation was hopeless. Wiping the vomit from her mouth, she made her way back to Poppy's side.

As she took hold of Poppy's hand, she began to sob, for

she realised Poppy had taken her last breath, there was no more to be done.

A traffic officer appeared at the open passenger door.

"She's dead," wept Harriet. "I need to stay with her." Gently, the officer took hold of her hand and helped her out of the car. He put his arms round her, holding her until she had no tears left.

Harriet sat in the back of the ambulance as a paramedic placed her in a neck brace. It could have been her driving the car. Earlier, it *had* been her driving the car. She shook uncontrollably as this hit home. A blanket was gently placed on her. She tried to make sense of what had happened, but the truth was terrifying. She picked up her mobile, hands trembling.

"Mike, something terrible has happened. Mike, they tried again. It's Poppy." Her voice trailed off.

A few days later, Deputy Chief Constable Jack Peters made an unannounced visit to Operation Chapel. He made a brief statement praising the staff and offering support to anyone who needed it. He referred to Poppy's death as a tragic accident, before dropping the bombshell that Operation Chapel was to be run down. He said staff should expect to return to their departments and day jobs within the next couple of weeks. The justification? No credible lines of enquiry to pursue in terms of who might be responsible and why.

Peters was tall, Harriet guessed maybe 6 ft 3, in his early

fifties, with short mid-brown hair that had just started to grey at the temples. She noticed that he was sporting an expensive Rolex watch. As he spoke, she wondered why she felt so angry and upset by his address. Perhaps she should have taken a few more days off. She was finding it tough to remain composed.

"Sir, I'm Detective Sergeant Harriet Lacey, I wonder if I might say a few words?"

He nodded curtly.

"I just wanted to start by thanking you all for your kind words and support over the last few days and to say I firmly believe we still have important work to do here."

Before Harriet could continue, the room resounded with spontaneous clapping.

"For my part, I feel a duty to seek the truth, to seek justice for the dead and their families and a duty to seek out and punish those responsible."

More enthusiastic clapping.

"Yes, progress has been slow, but we have made headway in the last few weeks. If we have learnt anything, it's that attention to detail is fundamental. Reinterviewing family members and looking again at the crime scenes has yielded new information."

"I also wanted to take this opportunity to pay tribute to a special colleague. I know you are all deeply saddened by Poppy's death. On a personal level, I feel desperately, desperately sad that I wasn't able to save her." Voice cracking, Harriet forced herself to continue.

"The only comfort I can take is that she was not alone when she died. My biggest regret is that I never got to tell her how much I'd grown to like her." A single tear ran down her right cheek.

"Poppy had her whole life ahead of her and in an instant it was deliberately taken. I don't know about you, but I feel I owe it to her to find out who is responsible and bring them to justice. This was no road traffic collision." Harriet felt her voice falter for a second time.

"Mr Peters, don't let Poppy's death be for nothing; let's make it count, let's demonstrate that we will not be intimidated, we will not be bowed, and we will do our utmost to see this through to the end."

The clapping was deafening. For now, there would be no more talk of closing the incident room...

As the room started to clear, Mike took Harriet and Derek Wynn to one side.

"Well done, Harriet, brave speech. Did you see the look Peters gave you at the end?" asked Mike.

"No, but I can guess it was like thunder?"

"Just a bit!"

"That was a strong speech, Harriet, but what you said needed saying, well done," said Derek.

Mike moved closer to them both and whispered "I've just had some really encouraging news. A DC friend of mine called to say he'd been speaking to a witness. The man was on the other side of the carriageway at the time of your collision. He says the other vehicle was an old-style grey Mitsubishi Shogun Truck. He says there is no doubt in his mind that the driver deliberately placed the truck in the path of your Fiesta." Mike looked angrier than Harriet had ever seen him.

"Is he prepared to make a statement?" asked Derek. "And did he get any details of the vehicle?"

"He's happy to make a statement, but didn't manage to get the index. He did see the vehicle make off at speed following the crash."

"So, we may be able to trace it?" Harriet was trying to sound positive.

"Maybe. It's a good start anyway," said Mike.

"I've been thinking, it was a spur of the moment decision on your part to go out that day. Mike and I were in the office with Nick, it was lunch-time, so the room was quiet. I can only think of five or six members of staff myself who were there. One of them may have seen something pertinent," said Derek.

"I do remember Poppy was with her friend Janice when I called her away," Harriet replied.

"I'll ask, as part of a welfare check. She's taken Poppy's death hard," said Derek.

"I nearly forgot, I've a message for you both from DS Paul Jones. He doesn't think the venom was imported, it has a distinct DNA profile and Customs have confirmed there have been no consignments of live mambas for over a year. Best guess is the snakes are being farmed in this country," said Mike.

"That's interesting, but how do we move this forward?" asked Harriet.

"Paul is going to see if he can identify any unusual purchases of specialist equipment, he's currently chasing down a tip from a reptile expert in Surrey."

"With all the chaos of the last seventy-two hours, I haven't had the chance to ask about the outcome of your discussion regarding Alec Brown, did you come to any decisions?" Harriet asked.

"We agreed the situation is complex, that we are not comfortable involving Professional Standards at this stage, as we only have part of the story and they are not known for their sensitivity. We've decided to try to persuade Brown to disclose more detail. We figure Brown will be waiting to see if we rush to involve professional standards, when he realises that we've held back, he may be more inclined to open up to us," Derek told her.

Harriet nodded. "Sounds a sensible approach to me."

Harriet wasn't keen to head home, she didn't relish being on her own. Although exhausted and in pain, she stayed late to finish her statement into the crash. Derek and Mike also stayed.

"Whatever's the matter?" said Derek, getting to his feet. Harriet was weeping silently at her desk.

"I've messed up big time, how could I have been so stupid? So stupid, so stupid."

"What the fuck?" Mike walked across.

"When I spoke to Ben, I used my work mobile. What an

idiot. There's a real chance they were monitoring my calls and now they know where the children are. Hell, what am I going to do? And why the bloody hell am I sobbing?"

Derek and Mike exchanged looks.

"Okay, don't panic. You're crying because you've just been through a really traumatic experience, it's a normal reaction to extreme stress and it's nothing to be concerned about." Mike handed Harriet a box of tissues and Derek put his hand on her shoulder.

"What the hell is happening to me? What do they want from me? What do I have, or they think I have, that's so important that they are willing to kill for it? Things are so crazy."

"You're right, the whole situation is mad, it's bizarre, but we are a team and we will get through this together, understand?" said Derek looking directly at Harriet, who managed a nod of her head.

"I couldn't agree more. Now, Sheffield and its surrounding area is vast. I think it's unlikely anyone would be able to locate the children from the little you did divulge. I tell you what, If I leave tonight, I can be there in a few hours. I can assess the situation, and move them if need be."

"Oh, my God Mike, I can't ask you to do that."

But Derek Wynn was already on the phone arranging for a traffic car to drive him to Sheffield.

"Harriet, please don't worry. I have this in hand. I'll keep you fully appraised, I promise," said Mike as he left the incident room.

"Harriet, there's no way it's safe for you to be alone. I'll drive you home and stay the night," said Derek. Harriet did not respond.

"By the look of horror on your face you're not keen on the idea?" he asked. "If it helps, I was going to add that we will pick up Rebecca Wood on the way."

"Oh my God Derek, I'm so sorry, I meant no offence, I'm just..."

"Harriet, it's fine, no offence taken." Derek took her by the arm and led her towards the door.

Next morning, Mike was on the phone bright and early.

"How are you this morning?"

"Not too bad, just a bit stiff and bruised," said Harriet.

"Thought you'd like to know Annie and the children are fine. Annie's smallholding is remote, I'm confident it couldn't be located from your conversation with Ben. But just to make sure, a surveillance team will be at the farm for a few days."

"How did you get authorisation for that?"

"You'll have to thank Derek for that."

"Well, you are my hero."

"Steady!" Harriet could hear Mike laughing. "I thought you didn't rate me?"

"I never said that... Well, not to your face anyway."

CHAPTER 15

Harriet glanced at the service sheet in her lap. *A Celebration of the life of Poppy Elsa Webster 1994-2017. Friday 4th August, 11 a.m.* Whichever way she looked at it, it felt wrong to be celebrating the life of someone who'd died in such appalling circumstances. She looked around her; the modest Norman church had begun to fill up, mourners jostled to find space on the narrow wooden pews. Those who couldn't find a seat stood respectfully at the back. Subdued chatter was punctuated every so often by a child's scream.

Sunlight streamed through the ancient stained-glass windows, light beams danced across the ceiling. Then the organ burst into life: The Lord is my Shepherd. Harriet gazed at the rafters, she could already feel tears forming. The congregation got to their feet as a small white willow coffin entered the church. It was carried by Poppy's brothers, with Mike, Derek and Nick. Harriet turned her head toward the incoming procession. The coffin bearers were visibly struggling with their emotions, all except for Nick, whose expression was blank.

It was Harriet's turn to read a poem. As she got to her feet, she leant against the lectern to steady herself.

"Death is nothing at all, by Henry Scott Holland 1847-1914." As she spoke, her gaze fell on the flowers adorning the top of the coffin. White roses and sweet peas. She thought of the slip of a girl who had inadvertently ended her marriage, how traumatised she'd been when they first met and how unwilling she'd been to have anything to do with her. And yet despite this, they had struck up a friendship. She would miss the kind, generous and open girl who greeted her each morning with a smile and a coffee. Harriet's voice faltered.

After lunch, senior staff gathered in the incident room. Harriet took her seat for the briefing. She had mixed emotions about work continuing so soon after the funeral. It seemed she wasn't the only one, the room was subdued.

The briefing started late. With no sign of Nick, Derek Wynn stepped in. They were informed that Nick had felt unwell after the funeral.

"Today has been a difficult one for all of us. If there is anyone who would like to be excused this afternoon, you are free to go." Derek paused, but no-one moved. So, he turned to face DS Jones.

"DS Jones, I'm hoping you have some results for us?"

"I do. The British Museum have finished studying the gold coin. They are convinced it dates to around 336 BC and is Macedonian. Gold coins were highly valued and comparatively rare during this period. Currency was usually bronze, with only a limited number of silver coins cast. They believe it's King Philip II who is depicted on the coin and that it was produced for the celebrations held in the Summer that year, the same celebrations at which he was assassinated."

"Did they give any indication as to the value of the coin?" Derek took the top off his pen in readiness.

"Yes, and no; such coins are rare and of historical significance, and as such, are difficult to value. They would not be drawn further than to estimate that each coin could be worth at least several thousand pounds on the open market."

"Indeed? Well, we've now established that all the deceased possessed a coin, but what does this tell us? Have we discounted that the coins were meant for the afterlife?" Derek turned to Mike who'd been specially invited to the briefing.

"No, Sir, we've not, it's just not clear what their significance is."

"I agree, it's really difficult to say. I mean, it could be the case that to hold such a coin meant allegiance to a certain group or society," suggested Harriet.

"Can you elaborate?" asked Derek.

"Well, I'm in the middle of some research, it's early days, but it does seem that the symbol of the sun or star was of fundamental importance to the Macedonian people, particularly at the time of Philip II, appearing everywhere: over doorways, on buildings, walls, and in artwork. I need to see if its importance changed at all following his death. I've got some more work to do, but hope to be able to report back soon."

"Okay, thanks. To be able to say for sure how and why our victims were linked would help to move this investigation forward." Derek turned to the note-taker.

"Note to myself to ensure that an action is raised in

relation to exploring this symbol and its significance further. Action to be allocated retrospectively to DS Lacey's team."

Harriet had half expected Steve Smith to jump in. Indeed, she'd only mentioned her research to lure him into a retort, but he'd not taken the bait. He seemed preoccupied.

"Okay, where are we with the DNA samples?" Derek opened his note book.

"Some good news: we've got a profile, low copy, but it does enable us to say it's a female of southern Mediterranean heritage. Unfortunately when we ran it against the DNA database, there were no hits. I subsequently spoke to Superintendent Lacey who authorised it to be run against Interpol and all other UK databases including the Police and the Military. There were no hits on the Military or Interpol database, we await to see if anything comes from the police. On the face of it, it doesn't seem to move us much further forward," said Paul Jones.

"Okay, noted, thank you. Keep us updated, will you?"

Paul nodded.

"Anyone else want to add anything? No? Well, thank you everyone. The next briefing will be on Monday, have a good weekend."

Just as Harriet was tidying up her desk and making ready to leave for the weekend, a hand appeared on her shoulder; it was Derek.

"Harriet, have you got a second? Join us in Nick's office, would you?" He pointed to DS Paul Jones.

Harriet followed him and he shut the door.

"Harriet, I wasn't entirely truthful in the briefing. The thing is, we have had the data back from the Police database and it's thrown something up that is both fascinating but also confusing. Firstly, I should say that when the samples were sent off, I asked the lab to look wider to include any familial or similar pattern DNA. Remember this is low copy DNA so it tends not to be as accurate. What is fascinating is that these samples threw up a handful of unexpected comparisons to your own DNA. It doesn't necessarily mean anything, but it's intriguing," said Paul Jones.

"Hang on a minute, are you saying that the DNA samples taken from the scene of Professor Grey's death match my DNA?" Harriet put her hand to her mouth.

"No, what I'm saying is that there were some similarities or likenesses that often occur within families."

"So, are you saying that it was a relative of mine who was at the scene?"

"No, just that there are some associations between your DNA and that found. It's fascinating, but it may not mean anything. I'm going to go back over the samples, to see if we missed anything, to see if we can find anything to help us explain it."

"I agree with you, it is both confusing and fascinating," said Derek.

"That's one way of putting it." Harriet ran her hand through her hair.

"It really is nothing to worry about, Harriet, it's a mystery to solve," said a smiling Paul Jones.

But Harriet could not stop thinking about it. The logical part of her brain told her similarities often occur in the field of DNA, but what if there was more to it? In the end, she concluded that she had no choice but to wait to see if Paul came up with anything definitive.

CHAPTER 16

Harriet turned on the television as she did every morning, but as she jumped out of bed to take a shower, something caught her attention.

"Good morning, it's Monday the 7th of August 2017. Today's top story: the apparent suicide of Chief Superintendent Alec Brown, found at the wheel of his BMW."

Harriet froze. In the background, the reporter was explaining a car had been found with a pipe fixed to the exhaust and the engine running. Coming to, Harriet grabbed her mobile.

"Derek, have you seen the news this morning?"

"No, why?"

"Turn it on."

"Okay... Bloody Hell, not for one minute do I think this was suicide... Leave it with me, I'll call you later. Make Mike aware, will you?"

It was late afternoon when Derek managed to catch up with Harriet and Mike. They met at a transport café on the edge of town.

"How did you get on?" asked Harriet.

"Well, I've had a very interesting day. I went to see the officer in charge of the case, who just happens to be an old friend of mine, Detective Inspector Gary Lamsden. I learnt that on police arrival the garage door was shut but not locked. The BMW's engine was running. The pipe taped to the exhaust ran through the boot of the car into the back seat area. The boot door was closed onto the pipe. Alec was slumped over the steering wheel. Next to him on the passenger seat was a typed letter in a plain envelope, not addressed to anyone. There was also an empty bottle of Russian vodka on the seat. Alec was cold to the touch; his skin had a grey tinge to it. That was the first anomaly for me. In my experience, victims of carbon monoxide poisoning look routinely rosy in complexion. I think it's entirely possible that Alec was already dead when he was placed in the car. The second anomaly was the empty bottle of vodka. Alec famously drank Southern Comfort and rather too much of it, or so I'm led to believe. It will be interesting to discover his blood alcohol level. And, thirdly, Alec did not type, he had a secretary to do that for him. At work, he only ever sent hand-written, notes which his secretary scanned and sent by email. So, if he was going to leave a suicide note, it would absolutely have been a handwritten one."

"I presume you let DI Lamsden know your concerns?" said Mike.

"I did, and what's interesting is he confided that the Deputy Chief Constable has been making a pain of himself all day. He appears exceptionally keen to get the investigation done and dusted."

"Did you discover what Alec's note said?" asked Harriet.

"No, we were interrupted, but I'm due to catch up with Gary again tomorrow, at the post-mortem."

Harriet got to her feet.

"Before you go, there's something else I need to talk to you about," said Derek.

Harriet sat back down.

"I went to see Nick this morning, concerned that you may still be a target and to see what measures have been put in place to protect you. This is really difficult Harriet, but I'm not sure you are top of the priority list..."

"It's fine, I'm fully aware of my husband's shortcomings. The truth is that he's currently out of sorts; sullen, preoccupied and distracted by a young DC. There's been some blatant flirting going on. I'm afraid Nick Lacey has only one priority, and that's Nick Lacey himself." Harriet was staring at the floor.

"Thank you for making that so much less awkward than it could have been. Anyway, be assured that Mike and I are working on a plan to secure your safety."

"Thank you both, I appreciate it."

"You're most welcome. Shall we say same place, same time tomorrow for an update?"

Both Mike and Harriet nodded in agreement.

It was about five the next day when they got together. Harriet thought Derek looked drawn.

"It's no secret that I detest post-mortems, always have, so I had to resort to the old chewing gum trick to deal with the odour. As usual, there were two parts to the procedure: the physical, external and internal inspection of the body and the tests, toxicology, and biochemical analysis etc. If you don't mind, I'll read from my notes.

"Body photographed, clothing noted, position of clothing noted. Clothing removed. Body searched for evidence of residues, samples of hair and nails taken. Body cleaned and weighed. Personal details recorded: male, forty-six years of age, strawberry blond hair, collar length, blue eyes, old appendix scar visible. Shears selected to open chest cavity. Organs removed one by one and weighed. Many and varied blood samples taken. Use of magnifying glass by pathologist to search for unusual marks. Puncture mark found with associated bruising on left arm, photographed and swabbed, requires further investigation. Stomach contents sent for analysis."

"Sounds as if there could have been foul play," said Mike.

"Quite."

"And the suicide note, did you learn anything?" asked Harriet.

"I did, but you are not going to like it. I cannot reveal officially that I know what it says without compromising DI Lamsden. And before I tell you I feel I need to state for the record that I believe it to be a complete fabrication."

"Stop playing for time, what does it say?" said a frowning Harriet.

Derek sighed. "In summary, it suggests that Alec has been sexually involved with you, Harriet, and that you recently moved onto a younger man but not without blackmailing Alec for huge sums of money he couldn't afford. Apparently, you are in possession of sensitive photographs of him with prostitutes."

Harriet put her head in her hands.

"You should know that I told Gary that this was a complete invention. I said you are the most loyal and dedicated officer I know. Wholly committed to your family."

"Thank you." Harriet placed her hand on Derek's.

"This is a bloody serious mess, a concerted attempt to frame Harriet, to get her out of the way. We are dealing with some fucking powerful and well-connected individuals." Mike's nostrils were flared.

"I couldn't agree more, and I've had the heads-up that tomorrow morning Jack Peters will personally order Harriet's arrest on suspicion of blackmail. By late morning, you will be circulated on PNC as 'Wanted.'"

"Bloody Hell! What am I going to do?"

"Do you trust Mike and me?" Harriet nodded. "Okay then, you just need to disappear for a bit while we try to sort this mess out," said Derek.

"I strongly suggest you don't go back to the house, they may already be looking for you. Jack Peters doesn't like to leave anything to chance, he will want to locate you before making his announcement tomorrow. Also, I wouldn't put it past him to put surveillance on Derek and me. For now, you'll have to buy what you need. I'll organise a rental car for tomorrow. It will be parked in row E of the retail park on the edge of town. The keys will be under the front offside wheel arch," said Mike.

Harriet left her car at the transport café and took a taxi to a nearby town. Here she booked into a Travelodge under her mother's maiden name of Robinson. Exhausted by events she went to bed, but sleep did not come easy and was fitful.

Waking early, Harriet showered, dressed and made for the nearest coffee shop. A large cup of black coffee and a couple of slices of toast later, she was ready to face the local shopping centre. Here, she purchased a travel bag, clothes, make-up, a dark brown collar-length wig and a large pair of sunglasses. Making a conscious effort to dress down, she bought jeans, T-shirts, and flip flops.

A little after eleven, Harriet picked up the hire car. A grey Mondeo. She drove just shy of thirty miles to a small market town and booked into an old coaching inn.

Feeling disconnected and lost, she decided to apply herself to something. She sent a text to Mike to ask him to post her father's note books, along with her CID diaries. In the meantime, she'd concentrate on the only notes she had with her, the ones she'd made when she first started Operation Chapel. As she read, she spotted a telephone number in the paperwork of one of the victims. It contained an unusual combination of numbers, which included the sequence 8888. She'd seen it somewhere before, but where? She read on until the same number appeared in the belongings of another victim, and another. Excited, she had an idea.

"Mike, it's Harriet. I know I'm not supposed to call, but I really need a favour."

"Okay, got your text, package posted first class. What can I do?"

"Thank you. Do you by any chance have any contacts with HOLMES in this force?"

"Yes, I know a couple of the trainers quite well."

"I need a search of a telephone number, is that possible do you think?"

"Under the radar, I take it?"

"Yes, please."

"I think that might be possible."

"Okay, thank you. I'll text you the number."

"I'll get back to you."

"Thanks Mike, I'm much obliged."

While she waited for Mike to come back to her, she napped. Her dreams were of her children, for she hadn't been able to speak to them for a few days. On waking, she texted Annie to pass on her love, and promised to ring in a day or so.

A few hours passed.

"Harriet, it's Mike, I have a result."

"You do?" she said sleepily.

"Yes, and you're not going to believe it."

"Go on, try me." She jumped off the bed.

"That number was a mobile number for a man called Troy Manning."

"Troy Manning, Troy Manning, don't tell me, don't tell me... Oh my God, he was the accountant found in his burnt-out house. He was part of Operation Eagle!"

"Yep, you are absolutely right."

"That must be the link that was referred to, it must, but what the hell does it mean?"

"That Operation Eagle is connected to Operation Chapel?"

"There's no need for sarcasm. Yes, no, there must be more to it than that, whilst we can't yet prove that our victims knew each other, we may be able to prove they knew Troy Manning or at least knew of him."

"They did?"

"Yes, I was going through my notes and I recognised the number. It's unusual, so I checked and each victim had the same number either on a scrap of paper or in an address book, a diary, or in a mobile. Just the number, no name. Mike, we need to find out more about Troy. We need to establish when and how he died, compared to our victims."

"What if it was fucking snake venom?"

"Well, then it's most likely the same murderer."

"You're right. I tell you what, I'll ask Derek Wynn, I bet he knows someone who can look for us."

"Thanks Mike, that would be really useful. Will you let me know what he says?"

"Of course, I'll ring you back as soon as I know something."

"Mike, before you go, has anyone approached you about my disappearance yet?"

"Yes, both Derek and I have had visits from Professional Standards; we were asked a few questions but not under caution, which was handy."

"I'm really sorry, they didn't waste any time."

"No, it's clearly being driven by Mr Peters, who seems in a particularly poor mood."

"Am I in really serious trouble?"

"I'd say no, Derek has already pointed out numerous flaws with the official version of events. I don't think it will be long before the evidence will speak for itself, just hang in there."

"What did Professional Standards ask you?"

"Well, it was fucking good luck the way they worded the questions. They asked if I knew where you were, and I said I did not, because at that time I didn't. Secondly, they asked if I knew where you might go and I told them I didn't have a fucking clue. They asked me if you had been in touch. I told them you had called me, and when they asked what we had talked about, I told them."

"You told them?"

"Yes, I told them the calls were about work."

"Mike, you're really mischievous. Did you piss them off a lot?"

"Probably."

"Well, I really appreciate your support."

"My absolute pleasure."

While she waited for Mike to update her further, Harriet began to think about Nick. They hadn't spoken at the funeral. He must know about her current predicament, but neither Mike nor Derek had mentioned that he'd been trying to contact her.

Smarting with indignation, she left the hotel to drive to a nearby supermarket for food and a bottle of wine. As she drove back, her thoughts returned to Nick. She wondered where he was living, whether he'd moved back into the family home. She couldn't resist driving past. Parking up around the corner she walked back towards the house, keeping herself tucked into the fence line, conscious that it might still be subject to surveillance. She tiptoed down the side alley and through the back gate. There was someone in the kitchen, the lights were on, and she could hear soft music. She edged her way closer, until she could see into the garden room. There he was, in the company of the young DC he'd been flirting with. Rachel something or other, she couldn't recall her surname. They appeared to be nearing the end of their meal.

Without warning, they began to kiss passionately. Harriet felt herself blush. She turned away, but something made her glance back and things had progressed. Plates had been pushed to one side and clothing was being removed at an alarming rate. Harriet fought back tears. With her heart beating faster than usual she knew in that moment Nick was no longer for her. Yanking her wedding ring from her finger, she beat a hasty exit, but not before she'd observed her soon-to-be-ex-husband thrusting himself into Rachel. She could no longer ignore Nick's behaviour.

Later that evening, she wondered how her husband would try to justify his latest encounter. And so soon after Poppy's death. She clearly didn't know him. Was this behaviour out of character? Was it possible to live with someone, share a bed, have children with them, but never really know them? She worried about what she was going to say to the children. How would they cope, where would she live? Where would they live? Would there be a hideous custody battle?

Thinking about her relationship problems just made her

feel sad and down, she would focus instead on her father's note books which had now arrived. One entry jumped out immediately.

Today, in a suite of rooms in the Royal Palace, we came across a significant number of carvings: on pillars, over entrances, in the cornicing. The most exquisitely executed images of snakes, or vipers, I've ever come across, all identical in design, but not in size. Carved into the stone and marble. But there is no getting away from the fact that this part of the palace feels cold and sinister, and I'm not the only one to think so.

Reaching for the bundle of papers Mike had sent, she selected a crime scene photograph. The tattooed snake was identical to the sketches in her father's note book. Now might be a good time to explore the historical aspects to this case, Harriet mused. She would travel to her father's old university first thing in the morning.

CHAPTER 17

On Kate's desk was a significant pile of laptops awaiting her attention. But instead she was staring out of the window. It was a beautiful summer's day, far too lovely to be stuck at work. As she glanced at the clock, her mobile sounded.

"Is now a bad time?" asked her father.

"You sound anxious."

"Do I? Well yes, perhaps I am a little. I understand from Cyrus that you are the model student: attentive, interested, a fast learner."

"For the first time in my life, I really feel I belong and what I'm learning is worthwhile."

"I'm so pleased; it was the right thing to support, rather than punish you. Anyway, I've called to ask for your help. Cyrus says you're ready. I'm going to play you a recording of a telephone conversation intercepted between Cleo and an unknown male."

"*It's me, I've found her.*"

"*Well done, but how?*"

"*With a bit of help from Steve Smith, we traced the car hire company and with the assistance of another contact, I had the car's tracker hacked. All I had to do was follow the car.*"

"*Bloody well done, Cleo. Where are you?*"

"*Sheffield University, the History building. I've had a good look around and there is only one entry and exit point.*"

"What the hell is she doing there?"

"Well I'd imagine what any self-respecting detective would do: following up a lead or seeking information. This is where her father was Professor of Ancient History."

"How'd you know that?"

"Well, I'm obviously a half-decent criminal who does her homework." Cleo laughed.

"Right then, I'll send some of my people to take care of this."

"Do you really think that's a good idea? Look what happened last time, it was a bloody disaster."

"Don't be a bitch, Cleo."

"Really? Really? You have poor recollection; I advised against using your inexperienced cronies. The last job was a catastrophe, sheer recklessness on your part."

"Whatever, but I'm using my people; hang around if you like."

"Bloody hell, Dad."

"We believe the conversation is about Detective Sergeant Harriet Lacey, wife of Superintendent Nick Lacey, you remember? The officer you sent the tape recorder to."

"Yes, and you think Harriet Lacey is in danger?"

"We do. Word is that she has helped to turn the enquiry into our friends' deaths around. It is now a multiple murder investigation, but someone close to the investigation is hot under the collar about this and wants her silenced. Harriet is extremely popular, tough, resourceful and intelligent. We can't allow her to come to harm."

"What is it that you want me to do?"

"You are to go to Sheffield with a small team and keep an eye on Cleo. You are only authorised to act if you assess that there is a danger to life. Cyrus will brief you. And good luck."

"Thank you, I can't tell you how much I appreciate being given a second chance."

"You've earned it, now stay safe please and do not underestimate Cleo."

CHAPTER 18

Harriet parked her car in a Visitor space. As she opened the car door, the heat of the day hit with full force. It didn't take long to find the History Department, she'd been to the eighth floor of the tower many times before. It was surprisingly quiet, but the absence of students was soon cleared up by the receptionist. Of course, it was the Summer holidays, this meant there was only a skeleton staff on campus.

It was less than five minutes before Harriet noticed a male sauntering down the corridor towards her. As he got closer she estimated he was at least 6 ft tall, well built, but not fat. He was wearing denim jeans, a casual shirt and beige baggy cardigan. His hair was auburn, layered and collar length. And he was clean shaven. As he got closer, Harriet thought he looked vaguely familiar.

He reached out his hand and introduced himself. "Hello, I'm Professor Andrew Hudson."

Harriet jumped to her feet. "No, really? I had no idea," she said.

"And you are?" he replied, smiling, but he looked slightly bemused.

Harriet did not reply; she was staring at the man.

"How can I help you?" he said with obvious amusement.

"Well, I've come to see you," she said, still staring at him intently.

"Well, you've got me," he replied.

"Good God, a Professor? Are you serious?"

"That's a bit rude," he said feigning hurt.

"There must be some mistake?" said Harriet.

"No mistake. And you are?"

"Ah, I'm Harry Lacey, but you knew me as Rayfield," she said.

"Harry Rayfield. No, it can't be, are you sure?" He was scrutinising the woman before him.

"Yes, of course I'm sure, it's just I don't usually look like this. It's complicated." Harriet removed the wig and ran her fingers through her hair.

"Oh, there she is... nice hair, that's much better."

"Well, are you going to discuss the merits of Doric pillars with me or not?" she said grinning.

"Yes, of course, but hang on a minute, it's starting to come back to me..."

"You're going to talk about the drunken incident, aren't you? I was so drunk that it took my roommate two days to move me from her floor to my room."

"And we..."

"Yes, um, well, I remember kissing you, kissing you a lot, and I remember you leaving, but I don't recall the bit in the middle. I was too embarrassed to say anything to you, and that was it essentially, the end of a great friendship. You were my best friend and I was too cowardly, too mortified to speak to you about that night. But if I recall correctly, you studiously avoided the subject and me as well," said Harriet, blushing slightly.

"I know. Well, I was embarrassed too. Suddenly I found myself snogging my best friend. It was confusing and I didn't know how to get back to being just friends again. It was easier not to speak about it and to leave and never see you again. And yet I have never forgotten and often regretted not putting things right. You know, I really am very sorry."

Unexpectedly, Harriet felt butterflies in her stomach; she took a deep breath.

"That's really good to know. But if you don't mind, we should get on."

"Yep, no problem, I will do my best to assist, come down to my office."

As she followed him down the corridor, she thought he'd changed little since their student days together. His sharp wit and his boyish charm were still very much in evidence.

Andrew's office was a large corner room, framed by windows, light and airy and untidy. Two large well-worn brown leather sofas occupied the centre of the room. A large desk ran along the wall on the far side; it was piled high with a multitude of papers and a heavy desk lamp. Every conceivable piece of wall space had been covered in framed maps and pictures and much of the floor was occupied by boxes containing an assortment of bone fragments and pottery. A man's room, thought Harriet to herself, as she made her way to one of the sofas.

"Okay," said Harriet after a short pause. "I'm interested in the period of Macedonian history around 336 BC, before the Persian invasion. I am keen to know more about the dynamics of Olympias, Alexander and Philip's relationships, about Philip's death and the aftermath."

"Okay, but it might take some time." Andrew gave a wry smile. There was a glint in his eye that she recognised.

"Well, how about you start and I will tell you if you are on the right track?" she said smiling.

"Perfecto, but first I must have a coffee. Do you still take yours with no milk or sugar?"

"How on earth did you recall that?"

Laughing, he said, "You had a huge effect on me Harriet." Harriet laughed too, but she couldn't tell if he was joking or not.

"Professor Hudson, stop flirting."

"Okay," he said grinning.

"Let me see, where to start, there are significant gaps in our knowledge, so some of what I tell you will be supposition. It's not disputed, however, that before Philip came to power, Macedonian society was rural and pretty unsophisticated, dominated by aristocratic families whose main source of wealth and prestige were their herds of horses and cattle.

"Philip II was in many ways a visionary, for he made a military way of life for Macedonian men. It became a professional occupation under him that paid enough to allow soldiers to be soldiers all year round, unlike in the past when they had only been part-time."

"I never knew that."

"Philip also allowed the sons of Macedonian nobles to receive education at Court. With the result that these young men developed a respect and fierce loyalty to their King. This allowed Philip to keep their fathers from interfering with his authority." He paused for a minute.

"Philip's marriages are interesting in that he was polygamous. He appeared to marry to strengthen his position. His first marriage is thought to have been to an Illyrian Princess called Audata; this sealed an alliance with the Illyrians, preventing an impending attack. Audata gave birth to a daughter Cynane.

"Next, he married Phila, princess of Elimea. Some believe Nicesipolis of Pherae in Thessaly was the next wife, and that she bore him a daughter, Thessalonica. Then in 357 BC he married Princess Olympias from the neighbouring country of Epirus. A year after this, she bore him a son named Alexander, later known as 'Alexander the Great'. She also bore him a daughter named Cleopatra.

"Philinna of Larissa may have been next. She bore a son, Arrhidaeus, later called Philip III of Macedon. Then Meda of Odessa, daughter of the king of Thrace, and finally Philip married Kleopatra, a Macedonian of noble birth and niece to General Attalus. Whether Kleopatra bore him any children is much disputed, some historians believe there was no time to have done so, between the marriage and Philip's death. But there are references to both a boy and a girl and some sources even name the boy. In truth, it's unlikely that we will ever know for certain. Are you still with me, or are you glazing over, like so many of my students?" he asked.

"No, I am very much with you." Raising her head from her note book she said, "This is fascinating. I only wish that I had listened more actively when my father used to talk so animatedly about Philip."

"Ah yes, the great Professor Rayfield. Incredibly knowledgeable, with amazing insight. He is considered this country's expert on Philip's reign. I presume you have spoken with him?"

There was a pause. "Sadly, no," Harriet told him. "He's now very poorly and suffering from a rare form of dementia called Primary Progressive Aphasia. It's debilitating."

"I'm so very sorry to hear that. Do you want a break?"

Harriet shook her head.

"The truth is that very little is known about the character of Philip, or for that matter, his domestic life. Contemporary authors showed little interest in Macedonian internal affairs. What we do know is that the procreation of heirs seemed to affect a royal wife's status."

"That sounds predictable," said Harriet.

"Well, we are talking about at least three hundred and fifty years before Christ."

"What about Olympias, what is known about her?"

"References to Olympias are rare; it's thought that she was nearly eighteen when she married Philip, as possibly his fourth wife. She is variously described as beautiful, sullen and arrogant, with a dangerous and violent temper. Some historians think that she enjoyed her high position because her son was accepted as the next in line to the throne. It appears the first-born son Philip Arrhidaeus was deemed incapable of succeeding his father, due to some ambiguous mental disability.

"Olympias is recorded as having a fascination with snakes and for keeping a considerable assortment of large tame serpents with her. She is also recorded as being a devout member of the orgiastic snake-worshipping cult of Dionysus. Some say she slept with snakes."

"What does that mean, slept with snakes?" asked Harriet.

"Well, it's not clear, but you are a woman of the world, use your imagination."

"You are joking! I mean that's really quite disturbing; this is not fact, right?"

"It's not clear what is meant by the sources. It could be myth, it could be truth."

Harriet shuddered; this was not something she wished to dwell on.

"Carry on, carry on." She was beginning to enjoy herself. By mid-afternoon the Professor has produced a couple of good bottles of Shiraz and some snacks which were improving Harriet's enjoyment no end.

"Historians Livy & Polybius suggest that the silver and gold mines, at Pangaeus, were the exclusive possession of the King, and allowed him to generate currency. It's believed that the King would divide the rewards of war between himself and his men. During Philip's and Alexander's reigns this was a considerable source of income. We are pretty sure that gold and silver loot, taken during the European and Asian campaigns, were smelted into ingots and stockpiled."

"Do you know, I think I'm very lucky to be alive today. For there is such freedom and equality of opportunity, far beyond the imagination of the women living in Philip's Macedonia. Western girls today can strive to be pretty much anything they want. And yes, there is still chauvinism and unfairness, but in many ways challenging this defines the modern women. Take the police service for example: for all its protestations of parity it is still far from that. If you're a woman who wants to get on, you need to be completely single-minded and focussed on your career. There is no room for diversions, and luck plays a huge part. If you have enlightened managers it helps, if you don't, it can be miserable. In my experience, female managers often become masculine to fit in, which is a great shame. Personally, I think 'ordinary women' are bloody amazing. Intelligent, driven, and yet also nurturing. It's so sad that society fails to appreciate those qualities. To me, many so-called successful men have lost definition. In truth, they are emasculated, cared-for, mothered and nurtured by their far more capable women. Many have lost that raw masculinity that once defined men."

"Harriet, I completely agree. The female species is tougher, by far the more resourceful and driven."

"It's okay, I've finished ranting now. You were saying?"

"Well, I think you might be surprised, there was a certain amount of 'girl power' even in Philip's time. Never underestimate the power of personality. Philip's first wife

Audata was trained as a warrior and raised her daughter Cynane in the same way. When Cynane was grown, she went to war with her father. As his oldest child, she is said to have considered herself entitled to inherit. And she led a mercenary force in the dynastic wars that followed her father's death. Cynane's daughter Eurydice was also trained to hunt and fight and took up the cause by challenging Olympias. The war that followed was said by Duris of Samos to be the first war to be waged between women. It ended in the capture and death of Audata."

"So, did things settle down between these two factions of warring women?"

"Good question, and one that I cannot really answer, for there are hints of discord and warring, but little actual historical evidence."

As Andrew talked, it dawned on Harriet that her father hadn't published the discoveries she'd read about in his note book: the coin horde, the snake carvings, the incomplete inscription hinting at a war between the women in Philip's life. She wondered why that was.

"What can you tell me about the sixteen-point sun I keep seeing everywhere?" she asked.

"Right, yes, sometimes it's called the Vergina Sun or Argead Star; it has also been referred to as a 'sunburst' or a 'starburst'. No-one agrees on its significance, other than it's been of importance to the Macedonian people for hundreds and hundreds of years and remains the emblem of the country today."

"Okay, thanks. Can you tell me anything about tattoos in the ancient Greek world? I mean, for example were they even common amongst the population?"

"Harriet, you are really testing me."

"Well, these damn snake or viper tattoos keep cropping up in my investigation and I just wondered if inking or tattooing was common in ancient Greece."

"I'm really not sure. What I can tell you is that I recall reading a piece by Professor Robert Graves in his Greek Mythology which, if I remember correctly, suggested that tattooing was common amongst religious groups in the ancient Mediterranean world. I also remember reading, but I can't remember where, that at the time of Philip's reign, it was most common amongst slaves. That does not mean to say that elite groups didn't also use them to identify themselves or reference themselves to a particular cult or belief group..."

Harriet was busy making notes.

CHAPTER 19

Time had flown; it was past seven and Andrew had disappeared to find chocolate and a bottle of scotch. Harriet was contemplating whether to mention the coins they'd found when her thoughts were interrupted by a loud crash followed by the sound of raised male voices. Jumping to her feet, she ran to the door, only to freeze at the last minute. At first she told herself she was being silly and it was just her old friend mucking about. But something didn't feel right. Slowly she opened the door and peered out. She saw nothing untoward but she could still hear raised voices. Had she inadvertently put Andrew in harm's way?

Closing the door quietly behind her, she grabbed the wig, her mobile and compact mirror from her handbag, before stuffing the bag into a desk drawer. She put on the wig and Andrew's baggy cardigan which had been hanging on the back of his desk chair. Placing her phone in her jeans pocket, she wiped away most of her make-up and put Andrew's reading glasses on her head. Heart pounding, she moistened her dry lips with her tongue before picking up a clip board and striding out of the office.

She walked down the poorly lit corridor. The door to one of the offices was ajar. Harriet hovered outside.

"Are you sure she's in this building?" said a male voice.

"Yes, totally, our source saw her enter this afternoon," said a deeper voice.

"And she couldn't have left?"

"No, so our source says."

"Dave, what is the Professor saying?" asked the deeper-voiced male. A third voice entered the conversation.

"He's being bloody unhelpful."

"Well, then make him talk, idiot."

Harriet sent a quick text, before striding through the door. There were two white males, possibly in their mid-thirties, holding Andrew's arms at the far end of the room. Nearer to the door she'd just entered by, were two other white men, one just over 6 ft and one just under. They looked younger, in their mid- to late-twenties.

"What's going on?" she asked.

"Who the fuck are you?" said the taller of the two men. Harriet recognised the deep voice.

"I'm Professor Hudson's secretary, Clare," she said, looking directly at Andrew.

"What the fuck are you doing here so late at night?" asked the same man.

"I don't need to explain myself to you. Anyway, what are you doing here? Come on Professor, we've got work to do."

"Well actually, darling, you do need to and he's not going anywhere," said the same man.

"Look, we don't want any trouble, we're updating student records. As far as I know, we are the only ones left on this floor." Harriet was stalling, looking for inspiration, a way to help Andrew.

"Well, we know different and want to ask your boss a few questions," said the man.

"Well, maybe I can help? What do you want to know?"

There was laughter. "Know Harriet Lacey, do you?" asked the man.

"Err, never heard of her, she certainly doesn't work in this department." Andrew cried out in pain.

"How did you even get into the building?" asked Harriet, doing her best to detract attention from Andrew.

"It was a piece of cake, we just picked pockets 'til we got enough access cards and then we swiped our way in," said the shorter of the two men. The others were laughing.

Andrew was now in an arm lock, discomfort etched across his face.

As one of the men walked past Harriet, brushing her arm with his, she pounced, knocking him to the ground. A second male ran at her and she decked him, but when the others pitched in, she was overwhelmed.

"You've caused enough fucking trouble, you have," said the taller of the men, rubbing his jaw.

"Dave, Melvin, tie her up and tape her mouth, her hands and her feet, make sure she can't move a muscle. Put her somewhere out of the way now!" he shouted.

Despite several attempts to escape, Harriet found she was unable to break free.

Within minutes, she had been dragged unceremoniously

into the walk-in cupboard in Andrew's office. It was full of human skulls, piled onto the shelving that dominated the tiny space. There were more in boxes and crates on the floor. The two men moved a couple of crates before placing Harriet on the floor with her back against the wall. They moved the crates back and slammed the cupboard door shut. It was pitch black. Harriet tried to move but she could not, so effectively had they trussed her up. She could, however, hear them talking just the other side of the door.

"That should do it. This is more fucking difficult than it was meant to be," said one.

"Tell me about it," said the other.

Then there was a third voice, a woman's. "Has she been found yet? Where are the others?"

"Fuck you," said one of the males. There was the sound of a scuffle, before the same man shouted, "Sorry, sorry, I didn't mean it."

"Harriet Lacey is a bloody nuisance," said the woman ignoring the man. "I personally don't think she knows half of what they suspect. But I do think they've underestimated her. In a way, I'm beginning to like her. She has guts, which is more than can be said for you lot. Have you any idea where she might be? She can't have gone far. I saw her enter and she's not exited the building. She can't have disappeared into thin air, now can she?"

Harriet sat in the darkness praying the men didn't mention they'd just put the Professor's secretary in the cupboard. Something told her this woman would not be as easily convinced as they'd been.

"What's her boyfriend the Professor saying?" asked the woman.

"He's refusing to talk," said one of the men.

"Oh, is he? Well, let's see if I can persuade him," was the stony reply.

Harriet listened intently to the 'click clack' of heels disappearing into the distance. A short while later there were raised voices, and a little later still there appeared to be two females shouting. Although Harriet strained to hear what the argument was about, they were too far away.

The cupboard was dark, dusty and hot. Harriet began to feel dizzy. It was almost more than she could bear. She began to think about Andrew, and her children, before she passed out.

Several hours went by before Harriet once again became aware of voices. The door to the cupboard opened and a beam of torch light fell on her. She took a deep breath and prepared to meet her fate.

"Hello, there, don't be afraid, I'm PC 1520 Guthrie of South Yorkshire Police. Mike got your text, it just took us a while to find you."

The voice belonged to a large mixed-race officer, maybe in his early twenties. He had the bluest eyes, short light brown afro hair and freckles. His open face was slightly shiny, Harriet imagined from the effort of crawling into the cupboard.

PC Guthrie found the light switch. Smiling, he squeezed his way across a crate and, lying on his stomach on the second, quickly set to work removing the tape from Harriet's hands and feet. Detaching it from her mouth was trickier, it stung like nothing else she'd ever experienced.

"Are you okay, Harriet?" he asked.

But all Harriet could think of was Andrew. "Can you tell me where Professor Andrew Hudson is? Is he okay?" She removed her wig and ran her fingers through her sweaty hair.

The briefest of frowns crossed PC Guthrie's face. "Um, I'm not sure I can answer that at this stage, sorry. Let me help you out."

"Look, I need to know how he is," said Harriet, more forcefully this time and showing no inclination to move.

"Hang on a minute." He disappeared.

A short while later, a man in a shiny suit appeared. He introduced himself as Detective Inspector James Moore. He was much shorter than PC Guthrie, a white male, with sharp pointed features and tiny eyes.

"I understand you were asking about Professor Hudson. Can I ask how you know him?"

"He's an old university friend. I came to see him for some help." This was met with silence, so Harriet tried again. "Please can you answer my question, how is Professor Hudson?"

"Miss, firstly I need to know what you are doing in this cupboard of skulls." Harriet didn't like his attitude, not at all.

She remained silent.

"How did you come by the bruise on your cheek?" he asked as he peered at her inside the cupboard.

Harriet put her hand up to her face; there was a lump underneath her left eye.

Silence.

"Is there someone I can call for you?" he asked.

"Detective Inspector, I'm not trying to be rude, but I'm worried about the Professor."

"Look, there's no easy way to say this, but unfortunately your friend is dead and I now need to find out why."

Harriet blinked, and tried to make sense of his words. "Oh no, oh no," she said softly as she covered her eyes with her hands.

"Look, I'm sorry, I didn't mean to upset you. It's just I need to know what you saw and heard. So far you are our only witness." Harriet didn't like Mr Shiny Suit. Overwhelmed, she wept quietly in the back of the cupboard.

Half an hour passed before PC Guthrie came back.

"Harriet, why don't you let me help you out of there? I'm going to pass a box of tissues through the gap, and a cup of coffee. Don't worry, I'm not going to try to reach you, unless you want me to," he said kindly.

A short time later, another face appeared at the door; a face Harriet had never been so happy to see.

"Don't cry," said Mike as he surveyed Harriet's mascara-stained face peering back at him.

"Oh Mike, I've made a hash of everything. You know Andrew never gave me up. It never crossed my mind, that they would really hurt him. For God's sake, who are these people?"

"I've no idea, but we will do everything we can to catch them. Now let's get you out of here."

Lowering her voice, Harriet said in a whisper, "If I come out, am I going to be arrested?"

"No, no, you've been completely cleared of any involvement in Alec's death. I sent you a text, but I guess you won't have seen it yet? I'll explain all later."

"What a relief, in that case, could you hurry up please, cos I really need to pee." Mike and PC Guthrie couldn't help but snigger.

A short time later, Harriet reappeared from the Ladies and made for PC Guthrie. She held out her hand. "Thank you for all your kindness."

"No problem. I'm Steve, by the way, good to meet you, sorry it's under such circumstances."

Professor Hudson's office began to fill up with senior officers; Derek Wynn had apparently been on the phone. About an hour later, the man himself appeared and Harriet felt a sudden unexpected urge to hug him. He made straight for her and they embraced.

A little while later, Derek handed Harriet his mobile. "It's Nick, he wants to speak to you."

Taking the phone, Harriet left the room and stood in the corridor.

"Harriet, where the hell have you been? I've been trying to get hold of you for days, what were you thinking?"

"Hi Harriet, how are you? Are you okay? Are you safe? I've been worried sick about you. I never for one minute believed you could have been involved in Alec's death."

"Well, yes of course, how are you? I really need to be brought up to speed."

Harriet sighed. "Nick, it's not always about you. Now is not the time. We do need to talk, but not now."

"I don't think you care about me anymore. I make one small mistake and you just can't stop punishing me, pushing me away."

"What did you say? How dare you, you sanctimonious selfish, selfish bastard. Don't you dare throw that at me, not now, not ever. What was the other night about? Sympathy sex?"

"I don't know what you're talking about."

"The other night?"

Silence.

"I saw you," she goaded.

"What do you mean?"

"I called past the house and..."

"Oh, it was just dinner, nothing happened."

"Don't lie to me. I saw you. Unbelievable."

"Rachel was just helping me to get over the funeral, nothing happened."

"Nick, that's not only untrue, it's disrespectful. You're completely out of control. I'm sorry, I really can't speak to you now." A flushed Harriet terminated the call and rejoined the others.

Once the debrief had been completed and Inspector James Moore had made an awkward apology to Harriet, she asked to see her old friend one last time. Derek took her hand and led her to the next office.

Professor Hudson was on the floor in a sitting position. His eyes were closed; he looked as if he were having a nap. Near to him were the two males who'd put her in the cupboard. They were tied to chairs, but weren't moving.

Harriet took a deep breath as she knelt down. Tenderly she smoothed Andrew's hair across his forehead. As she stroked his cheek, she began to weep again, for this was a man she'd been a little in love with twenty years before. For the briefest moment, she laid her head on his chest.

"I'm so sorry my friend, so, so sorry." She kissed him on the lips for the last time. Her insides ached, she felt drained.

As she rose, she was overwhelmed by the urge to hold his hand one last time. Slipping her feminine fingers into his large leathery palm, she felt something round and smooth lodged between his index finger and thumb. Tugging hard, she managed to wrestle it free. Wide-eyed, she surveyed the stone disc in her hand. Her sudden gasp alerted Derek and Mike who walked across. Derek gently placed his hand on her shoulder.

"Oh my God," whispered Harriet. "How did Scenes of Crime miss this?" She showed the two men the disc in her hand.

"It's not immediately obvious, I grant you," said Derek.

"Looks to me as if it was deliberately planted," said Mike.

Harriet turned it over in her hand. It was then that she noticed what looked like writing scratched into the surface. Examining it more closely, she realised it was a name: *Cleo Morris*.

"Mike, Derek, look at this."

"Blimey," said Mike.

"I'm going to get this checked out. I'll see if the name comes up on any of our police systems, but without a date of birth or further information, it's unlikely we will be able to make an identification." Derek took the disc from Harriet and left the room.

"I bet you anything," said Mike to Harriet, "the Professor was also the victim of snake venom. Then there are these two specimens here." He pointed to the two males still tied to chairs. "I wonder." He went across and felt for pulses. "They're cold to the touch. But, something doesn't look quite right. Look at their eyes, it's almost like they're trying to communicate."

"Do you think so?" Harriet moved in to take a closer look.

"Bloody hell, Harriet, tell me again about snake venom, the effects, how does it affect the body? Quick!" Mike was excited.

"Well, snake venom can cause parts of the body to tingle and become numb, or 'fall asleep'. Victims have difficulty speaking and breathing... Oh, my goodness, are you saying, are you saying, that you think these two men may still be alive?"

"If they are, it's barely. I'm wondering if someone skilful enough could administer an amount sufficient to paralyse but not kill." He stood up. "Paramedics! Now!" he shouted.

Several hours later they learnt Mike's hunch had been correct. The unfortunate males had been administered with a substance that had rendered them unable to move, but it had not been enough to kill them. They remained unwell, but anti-venom had worked and they were being guarded in intensive care.

"We may have just got our first break," said Derek. "We need to speak to them when they are up to it. I think we should book into a hotel and get some sleep before taking stock."

Harriet threw him a quizzical look.

"Your husband appears to have thrown in the towel somewhat and made me Deputy Senior Investigating Officer."

This was the best news she'd had heard in a long time. Harriet had worked with Derek Wynn before, he was an excellent detective: intuitive, honest and tenacious. She trusted him.

CHAPTER 20

They found a large sophisticated business hotel. It was just before 5 a.m. when they went to their respective rooms. Harriet's head barely hit the pillow before she was asleep. Twelve hours later she awoke with a crushing headache. She rose and wandered into the bathroom to run a bath. As she sank into the bubbles, her aching limbs began to loosen. It was from the bath that she made an important call.

"Ben, it's Mum. I'm so sorry I've not called for a few days, things have been crazy. How are you getting on?"

"We're fine, it's actually great here. Annie is lovely and she's taught me to drive her old tractor. It's such fun, I love it," he said excitedly.

"That's great, but are you actually helping or just having fun?" Harriet was laughing.

"I've been really helpful, I move animal feeds and old tree trunks and old sinks, basically anything I can find, and I've also used it to clear out the barns and to help move the sheep on the moors."

"Well, that's fantastic, and how's Amelia? Is she around to speak to?"

"Amelia's fine, Mum. She's not here, she's gone shopping with Annie, but she's been busy too looking after Annie's old spot pigs. She's besotted with them, and guess what? One of them has just produced a litter of piglets. She's named all nine of them."

"I bet she has. I'm so pleased you are having such a good time."

"Yeah, we are, it's a cool way to spend the summer holidays. Annie is so funny; mad, but in a good way. She has this habit of stopping us in the middle of a task. Sometimes she produces a huge tin of chocolates and insists that we sit in the yard and eat as many as we can in three minutes. I always win! Sometimes she creeps up on us to play a trick. Last week while we were taking a break she shot up from behind the wall with the water hose on full pelt, it was the best water fight I've ever had."

"In short then, you're in your element?"

"Yep, it's great, don't worry about us."

"Okay, well, give my love to Amelia and Annie, and take care. I'm very proud of you, Ben."

"I'm proud of you too, Mum, love you."

Relieved, Harriet slid beneath the bubbles. Her son was maturing fast. For the moment, she was reassured her children were safe and well.

That evening, Harriet dressed in a simple white shirt and jeans before meeting Mike in reception. They went to Derek's room. At the far side of the room stood a large round table overlooking the city, which was lit up like thousands of fairy lights. It was here that the three of them ate, burgers and chips washed down with several lagers each. It had been quite some time since Harriet had eaten and she was hungry.

All too soon the meal was over, and it was time to get down to business.

Mike was the first to speak. "Okay, deep breath everyone; we need to pull this fucking thing together, so where to start?"

"Well," Derek cleared his throat, "there's lots to discuss. I suggest we take stock of where we are and work out what still needs tackling and in what order. Shall I start with Troy Manning?" Mike and Harriet nodded their approval.

"Last year I dated one of the Detective Constables on Operation Eagle, by the name of Rebecca Wood. Of course, you know her, Harriet. Although no longer together, we remain on good terms, so I approached her and explained what I needed. I emphasised that what I was asking could be dangerous, and I warned her that there was already a female officer whose safety had been compromised because of events apparently linked to Eagle. I impressed upon her the need for absolute discretion."

Harriet liked Rebecca, but she wasn't too keen on the thought of Derek dating her.

Derek continued. "The official post-mortem into Troy Manning found that he died from smoke inhalation because of the fire at his home address. There was no evidence of trauma, but there was evidence of burning to the oesophagus. This led the pathologist to conclude that he was most likely alive and breathing when the fire started."

"Is it possible that the reason for his apparent inability to move away from the seat of the fire could have been snake venom? Or am I just being paranoid?" asked Harriet.

"I was thinking the same thing. I really think we should ask for the original pathologist to look again, to look for venom in the tissue samples he took," said Mike.

"Agreed. By all accounts, Troy Manning was a skilful accountant employed by the rich and famous, but also by high profile syndicates in the city. He specialised in tax savings, if you know what I mean?" The other two nodded.

"It seems Troy kept an overt client list, but rumour has it that there may also have been a covert list, the location of which remains a mystery. It's not clear if it survived the fire. The big question for me is why all our victims had his number? Rebecca made a search of the database for our deceased, to see if she could find any common links between them." Derek paused for effect; this was too much for Mike and Harriet who shouted together, "And?"

"And, it appears that all our deceased invested heavily in a property development scheme in London; to be exact, in Canary Wharf. Troy Manning was the accountant oversee-ing the scheme. It was difficult, but with the help of an informant, Rebecca managed to ascertain that their individ-ual investments were hefty, more than £10 million each. Which begs the question, where did they get that kind of money from? It also appears that the scheme was not pro-gressing as promised. Despite high profile assurances there had been no return. Yet it had been sold to investors as a certainty. Various well respected and high-profile individuals staked their reputations on a healthy return. Unfortunately, we have no idea who these individuals are. I'm guessing their identities lie in Troy's covert list. At this stage, it's impossible to guess the extent of his involvement in the scam. You will not be surprised to hear that the investor's money has disappeared." Derek turned to Harriet.

"I'm just wondering if you can recall exactly what it was you were looking at when you were so unceremoniously pulled from Eagle?"

She frowned. "There were several lines of enquiry, I'll need to consult my notes and get back to you." Harriet didn't want to admit that she was having difficulty focussing.

"OK, so let's move on. Following the shoddy investigation into your assault, Harriet, I had DS Steve Smith put under surveillance. Not via the usual channels, I'm slightly embarrassed to say, but using the old boy network, which of course means it's inadmissible in any court proceedings."

Harriet knew this was out of character for Derek. Desperate times, desperate measures?

"This is bringing back fond memories of my old CID days: the fug of tobacco, aroma of old spice, stale alcohol, and last night's curry. The days when our business with informants, or snouts as we used to refer to them, took place in the pub. The farting competitions, fuelled by the consumption of beer, whisky and bacon butties." Mike grinned at Harriet.

"Very classy," said Harriet. Mike rolled his eyes at her.

"Steve Smith is a clever man, but he's also hungry for power. We were lucky to get two breaks. First, Poppy's friend Janice remembered that on the day you went to see Professor

Grey's housekeeper, Steve Smith was in the incident room. Chances are he overheard your plans. And, as it happens one of the other detectives recalls bumping into him in the car park. He was on his mobile as you drove past. Our second break came when Alec Brown was found dead. Smith's behaviour became openly agitated, I'm pretty sure he had no idea Alec was going to be taken out. Anyway, we followed him to a pub in the town centre where he met with the Deputy Chief Constable. Indeed, they met on no less than four occasions in the week following Alec's death. We managed to record parts of their conversations, which saw Smith freaking out. The DCC on the other hand remained very much in control and reassured him things would soon settle down. Frustratingly, however, the DCC did not fully implicate himself. He did, though, instruct Smith to find your whereabouts, Harriet. It was after this last conversation that Smith began to pester Mike with questions about you." Mike nodded in agreement.

"The truth is there is not yet enough evidence to take any meaningful action against Smith and Jack Peters. We will have to bide our time."

"What concerns me is why the DCC was so resolute that Harriet should be arrested. Why be so involved at that level, why be so insistent? Unless of course you have a personal interest or stake?" said Mike.

"What do you mean exactly?" asked Derek.

"Well, his complete refusal to even consider that Harriet might have been set up, for a start. Then, the sense of urgency. Why not wait until the results of the forensic tests? Why the necessity to close the case? I think it was because he wasn't keen on there being any bloody forensic tests. The quicker the matter could be wrapped up as suicide and the car and body disposed of the better, as far as he was concerned. For then it would be almost impossible to prove Harriet's innocence and she would no longer pose a threat. What he didn't bet on was your interference, DCI Wynn."

"Mike, I think you make a good point. Peters was not interested in the questions I posed, luckily for us, and especially for you Harriet, DI Lamsden was."

"You know, I think it's time I had a confidential word with the Chief Constable, Mark Jones. We joined together... sorry Harriet, I know you disapprove of this way of working, but I really don't think we have a choice," said Derek.

"No, I'm all for making use of contacts and tapping associates, so long as it doesn't disadvantage others." Yawning, Harriet got to her feet.

Just then, there was a knock at the door. The hotel manager entered grasping a large brown envelope.

"This has just been hand-delivered to reception for you, Mr Wynn."

"May I ask by whom?"

"No name was given, but she was a smartly dressed young woman."

"Can you be more specific?" Derek examined the envelope.

Harriet was mesmerised by the manager's French accent.

"I would guess she was in her early twenties, with long dark, straight hair. Maybe 6ft tall, slim, wearing jeans and long black knee length boots and an expensive-looking long black jacket. And she wore a striking gold coloured pendant on a thick gold chain, with a jewel at its centre."

"She clearly made quite an impression on you," said Mike.

"She was most memorable."

Harriet turned to Derek. "The mystery woman?"

"Possibly, but I'm not sure that really makes sense, does it?"

"No, not really. I suppose it depends on what's in the envelope."

The envelope contained a mobile phone. Attached to the phone was a handwritten note, which simply said, 'Listen to this.' So, they did. No-one said anything for minute or two.

"Well, I'll be dammed, it's the recording Alec played to me in the park," said a frowning Derek.

"Yes, how could I forget?" said Harriet. "It's maddening, I recognise the other voice, but I can't put a face to it."

"I think I know who it is." Mike mouthed something to Derek, but Harriet didn't catch it. She saw Derek nod.

"What if I were to say Deputy Chief Constable Jack Peters?" said Derek.

"Oh, my God, yes!" said Harriet. "Oh, crikey, shit."

"Yes, exactly. I really do need to speak to the Chief Constable and urgently. For we have no idea who else may be involved. We are in the unenviable position of needing to treat everyone outside this room as a potential suspect."

Harriet glanced across at Mike who was chewing his lip.

"OK, we need to come up with a plan of action. Nick is back in the incident room overseeing the enquiries there and the surveillance of DS Smith. I will update him later. But if it's ok with you, Harriet, I don't want to tell him too much at this stage. I really think we should hold our cards close to our chests until we are sure who we can trust."

"I absolutely agree. To be honest with you, I'm really worried about Nick. I don't want to say too much, but I think he may have a drink problem. Quite apart from the obvious concerns of drink-driving and being fit for duty, I'm not sure his judgement is sound. I just need to figure out what to do about it."

Mike was the first to speak. "Harriet, it's an open secret on the room and staff have been looking out for him for some time, but it is probably time to do more."

"I'll take this to my boss and persuade him to organise an Occupational Health referral. He won't like it one bit, so before I do, I think you should speak to him," said Derek.

"I know, it's going to be a hard conversation to have. I've been putting it off."

"Mike, can you do some detailed work into Troy Manning, specifically around his death.' Liaise with Rebecca Wood, would you? I want you to oversee the re-testing of his tissue samples for the possibility of snake venom." Derek was going through his list of actions.

"As soon as possible, preferably tomorrow morning, I'd like you both to go to the hospital and speak to the two characters we found at the university. See if they will speak to us. The longer we leave it, the more time they'll have to get a story together. I don't want to miss this opportunity. Get as much detail as you can and then ask Nick to allocate any enquiries that come out to officers. I'll attend Professor Hudson's post-mortem. Are you up to this, Harriet? I completely understand if you need some time to grieve," he said softly.

"No, I want to help, but I won't lie to you both, it's hard. If you're happy to bear with me, I'll do my best."

Then, without warning, Harriet made for the door.

"Sorry, won't be a minute, please excuse me," she shouted over her shoulder as she left the room. She ran downstairs to the lobby area. It was now the early hours of the morning. The Night Manager was in his office.

"Sorry to disturb you, but do you mind if I ask again about the lady who delivered the envelope about an hour ago?"

Looking slightly surprised, the manager nodded.

"Can you describe her face at all, add any other details?"

"She was stunningly beautiful, large oval deep green luminous eyes. There was almost an olive tinge to her complexion; she had presence, if you know what I mean? She moved gracefully too and spoke in an educated way."

"Can you recall what she said?"

"She greeted me, said she understood we had a guest by the name of Mr Derek Wynn, she wondered if I would be kind enough to hand-deliver an envelope to him."

"Did you ask for her name?"

"I did ask her who I should say had left the envelope but I can't recall what she said."

"Is there by any chance any CCTV of the reception area?"

"Yes."

"Could I have a copy of it?"

"I'll bring it up to Mr Wynn's room as soon as I've copied it."

"Don't you want to see any form of identification?"

"Oh, no Madam, for I've just recalled what the lady said. When I asked her who I should say had called, she replied, 'All you need to know is that Mr Wynn is a police officer working on a very important case. I think he might find this useful'."

"Useful?"

"That's what she said."

Harriet sprinted back upstairs to the others.

Approximately ten minutes later, the Night Manager arrived with a copy of the CCTV footage. They sat and watched it in silence. It was frustrating as there was no clear image of the girl.

"I don't think she's the mystery woman," said Mike.

"No?" said Harriet.

"Although the description of the mystery woman and the lady at reception are similar, the mystery woman described by your attackers had a north London or Essex-tinged accent. The manager has described the lady at reception as 'well educated'. I take that to mean she spoke in a kind of BBC presenter way. Also, we know the mystery woman has a tattoo on her left wrist. If you look closely at the footage, there is a watch, but no tattoo."

Harriet rewound the tape to take another look.

"Thank you both, I think we've made progress tonight. See you at nine a.m. sharp," said Derek, yawning.

CHAPTER 21

Kate's mobile sounded. It was her father.

"Hi Kate, are you still in Sheffield?"

"Yep, heading back later today."

"I understand from Cyrus, that you had a trying time last night. He is full of praise for the way you kept your head and adapted the plan."

"Thanks Dad, I have to admit that I was far from sure that I'd made the right call."

"Well, we think you did and are all very proud of you. You made the best of a difficult situation."

"Thanks, I appreciate that."

"Now, I need to bring you up to speed: we have intercepted another call. It was made to Cleo at four a.m. this morning. I'll play the recording…"

"*Cleo, what the fuck?*" shouted a male.

"*What the bloody hell are you doing calling me at this hour?*"

"*What the fuck did you think you were doing? You're an absolute psychopath.*"

"*Oh, for God's sake man, shut up! They were absolute amateurs, idiots, they were making such a bloody mess of it. You should be thanking me.*"

"*Thanking you? Thanking you for what? You spectacularly*

157

failed to find Harriet Lacey and you murdered the only person who knew where she was. What the hell got into you? I'm reckless but you are far more than that, you're completely out of control."

"Peters, you're so naive and far too big for your boots. You think you're untouchable, but you're far from it. I may have lost my temper, but there is no come-back on you. Harriet will wait for another day."

"Will she? Will she? You don't seem to realise it's essential she's silenced."

"Important for who? Not for me. Seems you've got yourself in a bit of a fix. You should have remained loyal to me, you tosser."

"Sounds to me like Cleo has had enough of her boss. I wouldn't be surprised if she is planning to cut her ties with him," said Kate.

"I fear we may have to get more involved."

Kate was tired, drained of energy. The past twelve hours had been frantic. She was grateful to the team around her and to Cyrus, who'd prepared her well. But, in truth Cleo had scared her last night. There was an unpredictable darkness about her.

CHAPTER 22

After breakfast, Mike and Harriet made for the hospital, arriving just after 10 a.m. It looked like every other hospital Harriet had ever been in. Long grey monotonous corridors, the aroma of over-cooked food and stale urine. On the fourth floor of the main building they came across a private bay, just off the main ward guarded by two armed police officers. Inside, they found the two unfortunate males from the university lying side by side, eyes closed. They looked pale and were hooked up to a series of drips.

Harriet and Mike stood in the doorway studying the briefing note they'd been handed by one of the officers. So, these were brothers Melvin and Dave Cooke, aged thirty-three and thirty-six respectively. Dave had short dark brown hair, Melvin was completely bald. Dave was stocky, Melvin skinny. They were apparently East End boys who ran a garage and hired themselves out as muscle whenever the opportunity to earn extra cash arose. Both had previous convictions for theft, assault, and handling stolen goods.

"Good morning gentlemen, I believe you've been looking for me?" said Harriet.

Dave and Melvin opened their eyes and looked at her blankly.

"I'm Detective Sergeant Harriet Lacey."

Both men visibly stiffened.

"It appears you are none too pleased to meet Harriet then," said a grinning Mike.

"Aw my God. We're officially screwed," said Dave, turning to his brother.

Melvin began to sob.

"Look, we need to know what happened at the university yesterday, it may be that we can help you," said Mike in a more kindly tone.

Both men were physically shaking. Melvin continued to sob, whilst Dave repeated, "We're dead, we're dead."

"Look boys," said Harriet, "we need your help and you need our help. Tell us what happened yesterday and I promise we will do our best to pursue witness protection with the CPS."

Melvin stopped sobbing but looked vacant. He clearly didn't understand. So Harriet tried again.

"We will try to make sure you are safe. We will speak to the CPS, the Crown Prosecution Service, as they're the ones who make the decisions about prosecution, not the police. But I give you my word I will try my hardest to help you, if you return the favour and help us to understand what went on."

This seemed to work. Dave, clearly the brighter of the two, started to provide the narrative, with Melvin chipping in every so often.

"There were four of us – me, Melvin, Craig and his younger brother, but I don't know his name," said Dave.

As Dave talked, Harriet tried to organise what he was saying in her head. So, it appeared Craig had been in charge. His orders came via mobile phone. To help them to identify Harriet, a photo had been sent to his phone, but despite much searching, they'd been unable to find her. They had, however, come across Andrew Hudson in one of the offices and later his secretary, whom they now knew was Harriet and who they had restrained on the orders of Craig and placed in the cupboard. Then another woman had arrived; they knew her only as Cleo. Harriet stopped Dave at this point.

"Mike, do you have a minute?" They left the room together.

"Mike, did you pick up on the name Dave just gave?"

"Sorry, no, I was busy making notes. Why? Was it significant?"

"Yes, Dave called the woman who turned up last night, 'Cleo'. That's the name that was etched onto the stone disc I found in Andrew's hand."

"We should try to get as much information about her as we can, it might help us to identify her."

Melvin described Cleo as 'fucking scary' and unfortunately for him, his lack of respect towards her resulted in a humiliating physical put down.

"She fucking floored me and kicked me in the head," said Melvin.

"Cleo was dressed from head to toe in black: black boots, black jeans and a black leather jacket and T-shirt. Her hair was tied back in a ponytail. She was also wearing black leather gloves," said Dave.

"Yeah, fucking leather gloves," said Melvin.

"And carrying a large black bag," continued Dave.

"How come you remember so much detail about her?" asked Harriet.

"Cos she was sexy and, well, I was in bleeding awe," said Dave.

"Then what happened?" asked Mike.

"The big bloke, the one we'd been trying to persuade to speak, was sat on the floor of the office with his back up against a filing cabinet. Cleo knelt next to him and spoke quietly in his ear."

"Fucking quietly," added Melvin.

"I didn't catch much of what she was saying, but it was something about suffering at her hands, if he failed to cooperate," said Dave.

"Yeah, but then a bit later she changed her fucking mind, Dave," Melvin reminded him, his eyes wide open.

"How's that?" asked Harriet

"She lost her temper big time, after only about ten minutes. He just refused to speak, so she hit him around the head a few times and when that didn't work, she screamed he was a dead man. I honestly thought she was joking and I laughed, but she bloody wasn't, she opened her bag and brought out a syringe. She gave him one more chance to change his mind. He remained silent, he didn't even try to fight her off," explained Dave.

"Fucking brave or was it fucking stupid?" asked Melvin. Harriet shot him a look. "Sorry," he responded.

"She then stuck the syringe in his left arm and emptied its contents into him. It seemed to work quickly. I've no bloody idea what was in it."

"No fucking idea," agreed Melvin.

"But," said Dave, "within minutes he looked as if he couldn't breathe, it was awful to watch, awful, and then..."

"Oh yeah, and then another fucking woman arrived," said Melvin.

"A second woman?" queried Harriet.

"Yes, a second woman," said Dave. "Really, really pretty."

"Really fucking pretty," Melvin nodded.

"Can you remember what she was wearing?" asked Harriet.

"Yeah, long black boots, and a classy long black jacket. She was upmarket, if you know what I mean? Spoke like it too."

"And she didn't half shout at Cleo, something like '*For God's sake Cleo, what's got into you? Are you out of your mind?*' Cleo didn't answer, she just laughed. It made me shiver, really evil it was," said Dave.

"She knew Cleo then?" asked Mike.

Melvin answered. "Yeah, they knew each other alright. Cleo had a fucking vile laugh. It made all the hairs on the back of me fucking neck stand up."

"The second woman ran across to the bloke on the floor. It looked like she was trying to revive him, she seemed to feel for a pulse and I saw her inject him with something, but it didn't do nothing," said Dave.

"Sorry, did you say she injected him too?" asked a frowning Harriet.

"Yeah, she looked like she was really trying to bring him round," said Melvin.

"Anti-venom perhaps?" said Mike to Harriet.

"Maybe."

"But it didn't work, and when she got up she was shouting, she made straight for Cleo. When she reached her, she continued to rant and prodded her in the chest."

"Do you remember what she was shouting?" asked Mike.

"Stuff like *'How much did you use? You're completely out of control, you make me sick. Don't you have any boundaries? Are you completely...'*" He paused. "*'Pathi'* something," said Dave.

"Pathological?" suggested Harriet helpfully.

"Yes, that's it, then Cleo shouted, *'Oh shut up, what is it to you? You're not of my kind.'*"

"Don't know what that fucking meant," shrugged Melvin.

"Sorry, can I just clarify? She actually said 'not of my kind'?" asked Harriet.

"Yes," both men replied.

"Then what?" asked Mike.

"Then the second woman calmly said something like, *'No, thank God, even your kind would be upset by this. You've dishonoured your ancestors,'*" said Dave.

"Yeah, dishonoured your ancestors. Then it fucking kicked off," Melvin told them.

"Yeah, Cleo turned to the other woman with a face like thunder," said Dave.

"Fucking thunder," agreed Melvin. "I thought she was going to thump her."

"They went outside into the corridor, slammed the door behind them and all we could hear was shouting. Don't know if it actually came to blows," said Dave.

"Yeah, sounded like a real fucking barney," added Melvin.

"While they were fighting, Craig and his brother made a run for it. I think Melvin and me must have been in shock, cos we didn't move at all," said Dave.

"Rooted to the fucking spot we was. The fucking spot." Melvin shook his head as he remembered.

"So, what happened next?" asked Harriet.

"So," said Dave, "we were bleeding sitting ducks for the second woman. We tried to run but it was too late. She floored us and tied us to a couple of chairs. Then she took a syringe from her bag. By this time I thought I was about to be brown bread, and I was pleading with her, I mean really pleading."

"And I was shitting me-self," offered Melvin less helpfully.

"But she had a kind voice and told us not to worry, she said she wasn't going to kill us, just slow us down a bit. She had beautiful green eyes and it's funny, I did believe her. I only felt a little prick," said Dave.

Harriet couldn't help but break into a smile at this and kept her gaze on her note book to avoid looking at Mike.

"A fucking prick," said Melvin.

"Can you tell us how you felt after you'd been injected?" asked Mike.

"At first I just felt a fuzzy warm feeling, kind of like when you're happy drunk, know what I mean?"

Mike nodded.

"But then, I started to feel dizzy and my body was tingling all over, until everything went numb. I couldn't move at all, and could barely breathe, yet I was awake. When you came across to look at us, I tried to scream out to you for help, but nothing came out," said Dave.

"Yeah, it was the same for me too, fucking nightmare." Melvin shuddered.

It was lunch time before Dave and Melvin had finished their story. Despite the length of time it had taken, Harriet felt it was compelling evidence and that the brothers would make reasonable witnesses.

Harriet and Mike met up with Derek at a little bistro pub around the corner from South Yorkshire Police HQ.

"Well how did you two get on with Dave and Melvin Cooke?" asked Derek.

"It was an experience. Never in my career have I met a pair quite like them," said Mike, laughing.

"Oh really? In what way?" Derek was grinning.

"For starters, once we managed to get them to speak they didn't shut up, but my first impression turned out to be wrong. Initially, they came across as proper uneducated East End boys. But in their own way they had a sound recall of events, and were able to provide useful detail."

"Yes, I agree, it was slow going to begin with; they were quite a double act, and Melvin's politically incorrect asides slowed the whole process, but at the end of the day, we both agree they will make reasonable witnesses. What's interesting is that they referred to the mystery woman as 'Cleo' as etched on the stone disk, so we need to pursue this. But perhaps even more interesting is they claim another woman turned up and I think she may be the woman who came to our hotel reception last night. She is also the most likely suspect for planting the disk in Andrew's hand," said Harriet.

"It's almost as if she is trying to help us," pondered Mike. "Good work, you two. Well, I spent the morning at the Professor's post-mortem. Harriet, are you alright to hear this?"

"Thank you, but yes."

"It was pretty straightforward, as expected. The pathologist found a puncture mark on the left arm with associated bruising. It's too early to say any more. We should wait for toxicology reports. But I'll be mightily surprised if the cause of death isn't snake venom," said Derek.

"Well that fits with the brothers' account of where Cleo injected Andrew. Talking of Dave and Melvin, do we know what they were injected with?" asked Mike.

"Good point, and the short answer is no, not yet, but their blood is being looked at. It's intriguing though," said Derek.

"What about the enquiries to trace Cleo Morris, how are they going?" asked Harriet.

"Well, we've been able to narrow it down a bit, and with the information provided by our various witnesses we're now looking at someone in their mid-twenties, in the Essex and London areas. I'll let you know as soon as I hear something. Also, the local police are assisting with statement-taking of possible witnesses in and around the university. Statements have already been obtained from those who had their access cards stolen. Craig and his brother appear to be the main suspects here. Enquires are ongoing."

"Well, I think we have pretty much done all we can here for now. We need to think about going home. I need to see the Chief Constable and you two need to write up the Cooke brothers' statements. Mike, follow up with Rebecca Wood. Harriet, review the Eagle notes and files. We have a choice: we can leave now, or in the morning," said Derek.

"Give me minute, would you?" said Harriet, grabbing her mobile. When she returned, she was smiling.

"It's all sorted. If it's alright with you, we are going to see my friend Annie and my children. We've been invited to stay the night." She examined their faces, trying to gauge whether they were filled with dread at the prospect, but they both seemed to be smiling back at her.

"I'd be delighted," said Mike.

Harriet's mobile burst into life. She answered it immediately.

"Mum, is everything okay?" she asked. She listened for a moment.

"Mum, it's okay, just take a deep breath and tell me what's up. Mum, don't cry, it will be alright, just take it slowly." Aware of Mike and Derek, Harriet gestured to them that she would take the call in the hallway.

"Mum, do you have anyone with you?"

"Yes," gasped her mother.

"Well, hand them the phone will you, please?" Harriet could hear fumbling in the background.

"Oh Harriet, thank goodness. It's your parents' neighbour Mrs Morris speaking."

"Hello, Jean, how are you?"

"Oh, I'm fine, but I am afraid all is not well with your parents."

Harriet's heart began to race; she struggled to catch her breath.

"Can you fill me in please, because Mum's too upset to speak?"

Jean Morris had lived next door to the Rayfields for twenty-five years. She was the local Neighbourhood Watch co-ordinator, or busy body as Harriet's father used to refer to her. What she didn't know about her neighbours wasn't worth knowing. Harriet braced herself.

"Oh Harriet, dear, I am so sorry, but I think your mother has been hiding the true extent of your father's condition from you. Today, it just overwhelmed her. About an hour ago she arrived at our front door, dishevelled and distressed. I've never seen her in such a state. It was a shock, I can tell you. She rushed in and began to weep. It took a good thirty minutes to find out what had happened. Anyway, it transpires that George has been in a poor state for days. This morning he refused to get out of bed. Jane tried to give him breakfast on three separate occasions, but he wouldn't eat anything. Then, he suddenly got up, put on a shirt. Nothing else, you understand?"

"Yes, but it's not an image I care to dwell on," replied Harriet.

"Quite. Well apparently he just walked out of the house without a word. About five minutes later he reappeared with a couple of scaffolders. George was happy as anything and completely oblivious to his nakedness. Your mother, on the other hand, was mortified. But the workmen were kind and told her not to worry, they told her they'd pretty much seen everything in their job, nothing bothered them anymore. When Jane got George back into the house, he became verbally abusive and she lost her temper. I think she's probably sleep deprived, as it seems George rarely sleeps at night. Your mother has been napping on the lounge sofa as George refuses to let her sleep in the matrimonial bed."

"What about the spare rooms?"

"Well it seems in the last few weeks George has systematically taken apart the spare beds. Jane had no idea how to stop him. Anyway, it seemed less distressing to let him get on with it than to try to stop him."

"Thank you for your help, Mrs Morris, but can I speak to Mum now...? Mum, oh Mum, I'm so sorry, I had no idea. Why did you keep this from me?"

"Because you've had so much on your plate lately. This was something I felt I had to deal with alone. Besides, it's so personal and so unbelievably painful. I kept going until today. After George threw my third offering of porridge across the room, I lost my temper. I guess I just snapped. When I'd finished shouting he just stood in the middle of the room staring blankly back at me. I don't think he had a clue what my tantrum was all about. And then he put his old blue shirt on and left the house. I knew at that moment I'd lost him and that I couldn't cope any more. Harry, I am so tired, so tired." Her voice trailed off.

"Poor Mum, I am so sorry. Where's Dad now?"

"I left him sitting on a stool in the kitchen looking at the floor and muttering to himself. It's okay, Dennis, Jean's husband, is with him, they were always quite friendly."

Harriet spent another twenty minutes or so consoling her mother, before ringing her Aunt Maggie, who she knew would immediately jump into action. She relished a crisis and always had, it was a family joke.

It was a flushed and distracted Harriet who returned to join Mike and Derek.

"Is everything okay?" asked Mike.

"It's my father."

"Do you want to talk about it?" said Derek gently.

"I'm not sure I'd know where to start."

"Sometimes it helps to talk," said Mike.

"Okay, well in the last couple of years, the deterioration in Dad has continued at a pace. It's been heart-breaking to

171

see my enthusiastic, articulate confident father become a man who can no longer read, no longer follow the cricket or rugby on television. No longer write meaningful sentences or take part in conversations. Very occasionally, there are moments when he can make himself understood. Recently, he appears to have given up, just sits for hours in his chair. I guess the effort is too much."

Mike handed Harriet a glass of wine.

"It wasn't that long ago that he was a smart man, he took great pride in his appearance. Now he's shabby and dishevelled. His clothes are thread-bare and often splashed with food. He no longer strides along with purpose, but shuffles."

Derek put his hand on Harriet's. She continued. "We've witnessed at first hand the utter chaos surrounding his medication. There has been little discernible help. Although Dad attends regular assessments and GP appointments, his care has almost completely fallen to Mum. You would think they'd be offered social care assistance, but no, not unless they pay for it. Today, Mum reached breaking point. I've called Aunt Maggie, my Mum's sister, and she's on her way to rescue Mum. I need to go home, but I also need to see my children. I feel utterly torn."

"Well, if you'll forgive me for speaking my mind, to me it's simple: your parents are safe and being cared for by friends and family. Your children are the priority. You have the ideal opportunity to satisfy yourself that they are happy and safe, then you can go and deal with your parents' situation," said Mike.

"I absolutely agree," nodded Derek.

Decision made, they left the pub and went back to the hotel to gather their belongings. As a precaution, they changed their hire car before setting off.

Annie Gitting's smallholding consisted of a series of out-buildings and an old stone farm house. It was set in thirty acres and situated a few miles outside Sheffield. Built in the 1800s, the farm nestled in a dip on the edge of moorland, sheltered by a small copse of pine trees.

It was dark when they arrived. Annie met them on the door step. A good-looking woman in her early fifties, large framed, or as she liked to say, 'well covered', with an open and happy face. Her fairish hair, now speckled with grey, was piled on top of her head, in a kind of topknot. She was wearing her trademark apron. On seeing Harriet she let out a squeal of delight; this brought Ben and Amelia running from the other room. There was much hugging and shaking of hands. Harriet looked on with pride as her son manfully introduced himself. Only a matter of weeks before, he'd been an angry monosyllabic teenager. She had never seen him looking so well and so happy. Amelia too was different, taller and more self-assured.

Annie was a wonderful cook. Wild boar paté with homemade onion relish was followed by home-reared beef, roast potatoes, and home-grown vegetables. A huge Victoria Sandwich with ice-cream and custard rounded the meal off.

After dinner, they retired to the lounge to play cards, chat and sample Annie's damson gin and hedgerow vodka.

As they left the next morning Harriet realised her children were happy and settled and clearly in no hurry to return home.

CHAPTER 23

Mike dropped Harriet off at her parents' house. It was the only place she could think of to go, since Nick had moved back to the family home. Besides, she needed to check on her mother and find out about her father. She spent an uncomfortable night on one of George's old camp beds. George, it seemed, had been admitted to hospital for observations. Apparently, the ambulance crew had been most apologetic, but try as they might, they'd been unable to organise for the Mental Health Team to make a house visit. In the end, George went to hospital with a suspected water infection.

The following afternoon, Harriet returned to the family home to gather some belongings. As she approached the house, her stomach muscles constricted. Parking around the corner, she finished her journey on foot. As she reached the house, she noticed she'd begun to shake. Pausing for a moment, she told herself not to be so silly. Nick would be at work, she could let herself in, get what she needed and leave without any contact. Still, something made her ring the doorbell. She waited for a minute and had just put her key in the lock when Nick opened the door. Startled, Harriet jumped back, key still in the lock. Nick stood in the doorway dressed only in a towel. In the background, she thought she heard a female's voice call out.

"Hi Harry, how are you?" he slurred.

"I'm okay. I thought you'd be in the office. Have you been drinking?"

"Just a little," came the slightly hesitant reply.

"Nick, it's quarter past two in the afternoon, and you've quite clearly had more than a little."

"It's not a problem, I finished early," he slurred.

"We need to talk about your drinking."

"Do we? Do we really? And let me guess, you've appointed yourself as my very own alcohol counsellor?" he shouted.

"Let's not do this on the door step, Nick."

"Why not? You've clearly come here for a fight. Yes, I drink a bit more than I probably should, but it's not a problem, so bloody lay off me."

"Nick, you drink all the time. Don't think I haven't noticed the hip flask, and I'm by no means the only one."

"Oh, shut up. You witch."

"Really? Really? You do want to do this here and now?"

"No, not now," came the slurred reply.

"Look, I just need to collect a few clothes and other personal items."

"Right, bit awkward. I have a guest."

"I know you do, I heard her call out to you."

"Great, here comes the lecture on sexual impropriety," he goaded.

Harriet looked to the ceiling and sighed. "Not today, Nick. My clothes and bits and pieces are in the spare room. It won't take a minute."

Pushing past, Harriet walked into the hallway and sprinted upstairs. When she returned, Nick was still standing by the front door.

"Look, I'll ring you tomorrow at six," he said as Harriet made for the door.

"Make it seven," said Harriet. "I need to visit Dad."

"Well, I can ring you at your Dad's, can't I?" he said petulantly.

"You could, but he's not there, he's in the hospital."

"Sorry, I didn't know."

"Until tomorrow then."

As Harriet turned to go, she caught a glimpse of someone on the stairs. She paused to take a closer look. The girl was wrapped in a bed sheet and was holding a champagne flute. Her hair was pinned artistically on the top of her head. She was grinning, no doubt amused by the sparring taking place in the hallway. Noticing Harriet's gaze, she turned and walked back upstairs. There was no ignoring the enormous writhing serpent, running the whole length of her back. Recoiling, Harriet almost ran to the front door. A blushing Nick let her out. As she brushed past, she couldn't help herself.

"Nick, you really are a first-class dick," she hissed.

Struggling back to the car with the items she'd taken from the house, she rummaged through the glove box to find some pain killers for her thumping head. She had no idea how much time passed before she felt well enough to drive. Harriet knew she must talk to Mike and Derek about what she'd just witnessed.

Nick's phone call never came, and Harriet was not inclined to chase him. The whole situation was just too difficult. She chose to leave it until she had more time and energy, knowing full well any conversation with him would almost certainly turn into an argument.

After a short stay in A&E, George had been moved to one of the hospital's two mixed geriatric wards on the fourth floor of the tower block. Harriet went to visit later the same day. Having taken the lift to the fourth floor she used the hand sanitizer mounted next to the door to Abbey Ward. Pressing the buzzer, she waited for the door to open and then made her way to the Nurses' Station. After a couple of minutes, a large nurse with a broad Caribbean accent came across to greet her.

"Good evening, how can I help you?" the nurse said, smiling broadly.

"Good evening, I've come to visit my father."

"No problem, what's his name?"

"George Rayfield." As Harriet uttered his name, she noticed the nurse's expression change to one of revulsion.

"I'm sorry, is there a problem?" asked Harriet.

"Oh, no, not really dear, it's just your father has kept us busy, he's been a bit challenging," came the reply.

"Really? What's he been up to?" Harriet wondered what her usually mild-mannered father could have done to elicit such a negative response.

"Well, unfortunately he kept pulling out his lines. You know, his drips?" Harriet nodded. "He also threw off his bed clothes and his pyjamas and walked naked around the ward, before attempting to join several female patients in their beds."

"Poor Dad, he must have been so confused." Harriet noticed the nurse was still pulling a face.

"Look, he has dementia, he's poorly. Isn't it possible that the shock of coming into a strange place exacerbated his condition?" she asked.

The nurse shrugged her shoulders.

"Have you much experience of dealing with dementia patients?" Harriet's hands were now on her hips.

"No, not really. Follow me please." The nurse turned away. Harriet took a deep breath to control the anger that was rising within. Now was not the time to make a scene, she would pursue it later.

She followed the nurse to a side room at the back of the Nurses' Station. George was lying in a bed covered by a thin sheet, his eyes closed. There was a drip in his right arm and Harriet could see a colostomy bag hooked to the side of the bed. The room smelt; it was a shock to realise that her father was incontinent. The scene was in stark contrast to her mother's description the day before, of George being conscious and moving around.

Harriet walked across to her father's bedside and took his thin hand in hers. His nails were long and dirty, his white beard unkempt.

"Daddy, it's me, Harriet. It's so good to see you. Do you think you could open your eyes for me? Just for a minute? Please try, please." But there was no response.

George's skin felt cold and clammy. By now the nurse had disappeared. As Harriet looked around the small bare room she noticed an untouched glass of water on the bedside cabinet. Next to this, a forlorn plate of untouched food. A cold sausage, grey mashed potato and a spoonful of peas. Harriet tried again to rouse her father, but he did not respond. Finding a blanket in a cupboard she laid it across him.

An hour later, the stench was too much, and Harriet left the room for some respite. She went straight to the Nurses' Station to speak to the senior nurse on duty. She discovered her father had been sedated because of his erratic behaviour and obvious distress. Despite this, Harriet raised concerns about the level of sedation, as well as the uneaten food and lack of personal hygiene afforded him. The nurse promised to get the situation reviewed. Furthermore, she promised to get one of the doctors to make contact.

The nurse remained breezily optimistic about George's prognosis, explaining he was on antibiotics for his kidney infection. She told Harriet that one of the hospital Social Workers was actively looking for a care facility capable of dealing with his complex dementia needs.

Over the next few days, notwithstanding her punishing schedule, Harriet visited her father daily. But on each occasion she found the same depressing conditions. She was given the same assurances by staff that her father was getting the best care and was doing well. But this just did not marry up with her own observations.

Each morning before breakfast she would ring the ward, but this soon became farcical as the update was always the same. She would be told her father had slept comfortably and was sitting in his chair eating his porridge. Yet each time she visited, he was lying semi-conscious in bed.

Harriet left on the Friday evening feeling downhearted. She knew this was not the right environment for him, but it seemed there was nowhere more suitable. In short, the hospital did not have the capability to deal with such a complex dementia patient. Harriet suspected it was common practice to sedate difficult patients. She prayed the nightmare would soon be over, that her father would be discharged to a specialist facility, somewhere he would be treated with the dignity and respect he so richly deserved.

CHAPTER 24

Kate used her key to let herself into her father's flat. Each time she entered she was reminded of her mother. She paused to take in the scent of the roses that filled the hallway. On the one hand, she found it reassuring, it reminded her of her childhood. On the other, it provoked a profound sense of loss. She put her bag on the hall table, admiring the flower arrangement, and made her way to the kitchen. On the work top she found a note.

Kate, make yourself at home. Bottle of white wine in the fridge, help yourself. Could you please open the windows in the lounge and put the oven on? I'll be back about six. Thanks, love Dad xx

Pouring herself a generous glass of wine, she wandered around the large flat surveying the many photographs. She paused to look at the black and white photograph of her parents on their wedding day. They looked so happy. She wondered if she would ever be lucky enough to find a soul mate. And yet, the reality for her father had been heartbreak.

She admired her father immensely, more so since spending time with Cyrus. Kate had become close to Cyrus, she regarded him as her saviour, for he'd rescued her from the wrath of the Guardians. In many ways it was his influence that had helped to turn her life around. In a few short months, she had grown up. She was far less impulsive, less reactionary, and more confident. For the first time since primary school, she had a sense of belonging and a sense of purpose. It was early days, but she did feel she was on the right path.

Just then her father returned, dressed in tennis whites and glowing with the obvious effort he'd put into his game. He was smiling broadly. He scooped his daughter up in a bear hug and kissed her enthusiastically on both cheeks before running off to shower.

The doorbell rang. It was Cyrus, wearing a light-weight beige suit in homage to the fine weather and clutching a bottle of wine. He embraced Kate.

When Kate's father emerged, Kate and Cyrus were sitting on the sofa, glasses of wine in hand, looking through old photograph albums and laughing at early pictures of Kate.

After dinner they went out onto the balcony, where Cyrus lit one of his legendary cigars. As he exhaled, a plume of perfumed smoke snaked into the night air.

"That was delightful old boy, but I'm afraid we now need to turn our attention to business. Kate, we've intercepted yet another phone call to Cleo. And your Dad and I are of opinion that we cannot ignore it."

"Indeed." Her father looked serious.

"I suggest we listen to it first, then we can talk about it," said Cyrus. He set the recording to play.

"Hello?"

"Cleo?" said a male voice.

"Maybe, depends who's asking."

"My name's Clive, I understand you work for Mr Peters? I work for his boss."

"Well, yes and no, I'm not sure if I still work for Peters. How can I help you?"

"Well, I wondered if you might like to do some work for my boss instead? We have a couple of jobs lined up that require your particular skill set."

"I don't suppose there is any point in asking who your boss is?"

"That's absolutely right. But I can assure you my boss is decidedly more discreet and restrained than yours."

"Well that's refreshing. To be honest, I could do with a change, but my interest will depend on the terms and conditions."

"Six hundred thousand, a third upfront. The remainder when the jobs are successfully completed."

"On the face of it that sounds most generous, but of course I need to know the detail before I make any decisions."

"I quite understand. Look in the glove box of your Range Rover. You'll find an envelope and, if you decide to go ahead, you will be required to sign a contract."

"Oh, bloody hell," Kate exclaimed.

"That's one way of putting it," chuckled Cyrus.

"From what we've already heard I don't think there is much doubt Cleo won't take up this offer, which means that she will have access to better resources and be afforded greater protection; she's essentially been promoted. It also means that we should probably keep closer tabs on her." Kate's father was frowning.

"What concerns me is Harriet Lacey. Our intelligence suggests she is still considered a significant threat. Cleo's current boss has failed to neutralise her. I think more connected individuals are now likely to step in. I don't think we have any choice but to warn the police," said Cyrus.

"Really? There's no other way?" asked Kate.

"I don't think so, Harriet is too exposed. To do nothing would be wrong." Cyrus drew heavily on his cigar. "The more I learn of Harriet Lacey, the more I think she's quite remarkable. Despite everything, she continues to strive for the truth with seemingly little regard for her own safety."

"Certainly, she does come across as single-mindedly determined. But what concerns me is what happens if the police ever discover we had pertinent information and didn't pass it on. Isn't that an offence of some sort?" Kate looked directly at both men.

"I completely see where you are coming from and yes, you are probably right, but we cannot afford to risk exposing our organisation. Anonymity is at the very core of our existence. Our rules do not allow for disclosure. So, although it's a somewhat risky strategy, I'm hoping we can assist at arm's-length." Cyrus was pacing up and down the balcony.

"With that in mind, Kate, could you, would you use your computer skills to send an untraceable email to the officer in charge of the investigation, Nick Lacey? And warn him about the risk to Harriet?" implored her father.

"Well, yes, if you really think this is the best way?"

"We do," said both men in unison.

CHAPTER 25

A cold shower and several cups of strong coffee hadn't made Harriet feel any more alert. Her head was fuzzy and she couldn't remember the last time she'd had a restful night's sleep. But, as her colleagues began to arrive in the incident room that morning, she could see she was not alone. What a sorry bunch they looked. Some were nursing coffees, others surreptitiously taking tablets, and most were yawning and stretching.

"Thank you all for giving up your Saturday morning. A great deal has happened in the last week and we really need to make sure you are all up to speed. It's really important that we keep the momentum going," said a haggard-looking Nick Lacey.

Mike arrived late and took the seat next to Harriet.

"I'd like to start with the investigation into Poppy's death. Steve, can you provide an update please?" Nick didn't try to hide his aversion.

Mike turned to Harriet and whispered, "Bloody clever of Derek to suggest that Steve Smith be given these enquiries. It keeps him close, it keeps him busy. Look at how uncomfortable he is."

Mike was right, he looked drawn, tired and ill at ease. He was no longer the over-confident man who'd greeted Harriet on her first day on Operation Chapel.

"Well, er, yes, we continue to take statements from witnesses and to view dashboard videos. We are also looking at CCTV footage to see if we can locate the offending vehicle both prior to and after the collision."

"And has anything significant or helpful come from your enquiries so far?" asked Nick. Harriet thought he looked frustrated by the lacklustre update.

"Um, well it's early days. It seems that there was only one person in the offending vehicle but descriptions are poor; the Mitsubishi had heavily tinted glass. We know that following the collision the vehicle was seen to head at speed in the direction of Eastleigh Industrial Estate, but we've drawn a blank after that."

"Okay, well, continue as you are and let me know if anything noteworthy comes to light," said Nick tersely, before turning to Derek.

"Derek, can you update us with the latest developments on Chapel please?"

"Yes, no problem. Late last night we had confirmation that cause of death for Andrew Hudson was black mamba snake venom. We are confident now that our murderer is the mysterious Cleo. We also think she is responsible for the other deaths, on the basis that it's such an unusual modus operandi; the likelihood of there being more than one assassin using this method is extremely unlikely."

"But the question is, is she working alone?" said Nick.

"Yes, indeed, I'm not sure we know that yet. We're seemingly no closer to discovering who else is involved."

"What about Alec Brown? Do we yet know how he died?" asked Mike.

"We do. I can categorically tell you that he did not die from carbon monoxide poisoning, in fact he was already dead when he was placed in the car. He also died from an injection of black mamba venom. DS Jones confirmed this early this morning," said Derek.

With this news Harriet noticed the room come to life; many of her colleagues were now sitting forward on their seats actively taking notes, the room filled with chatter.

"Sir, were there any forensics at either the scene of Alec's death or at the University?" asked Harriet, looking at Derek.

"Unfortunately not. Alec's car was completely sterile. No hair, fingerprints, fibres etc. At the university, there were numerous fingerprints, including those of Dave and Melvin Cook, the Professor and you, Harriet. But there was nothing else of note."

"Do we yet know what Dave and Melvin were injected with?" Harriet asked.

"We do. A synthesised drug designed to mirror snake venom. Luckily for Dave and Melvin the antidote worked, so closely did the manufactured drug mirror the real thing. Also, there was evidence of an antidote being administered to Professor Hudson."

"Thanks Derek. Now, Mike, how are you getting on with tracking down the mysterious Cleo? I think I'm right in saying that we now have a possible surname, is that right?" asked Nick.

"Yes, Sir. 'Morris', a stone disc identical to the one we found in Professor's Grey's pocket and subsequently in the possession of the other victims, was found with Professor Hudson's body. The name *Cleo Morris* had been scratched onto the reverse by someone. Now, in their account Dave and Melvin refer to the woman responsible for Andrew Hudson's death as Cleo, so it would be logical to assume that *Morris* is her surname. From their descriptions of Cleo, we narrowed the field to a handful of women on PNC aged in their mid- to late-twenties. But I think I may have found the Cleo we are looking for. Yesterday, I took a statement from the Headteacher of an expensive boarding school in Essex. Let me read you the most pertinent parts...

'Cleo Morris, or to be absolutely correct, Cleopatra Morris, born 06/06/1991, was a student with us for six terms. Aged thirteen when she arrived and fifteen when I permanently excluded her. She is by far the most challenging student I've come across in a long career. Many of the staff and students were terrified of her. I remember her as a manipulative, spiteful bully. If I'm honest, the only reason she was with us for so long was down to her persuasive parents and their generous donations to the school. She was very much a loner and a prolific reader of thrillers. A gifted linguist too, spoke at least three languages fluently. Highly intelligent. Anyway, we parted company when her pet snake escaped. When we failed to locate the serpent, we were forced to enlist the assistance of the RSPCA who eventually located it down the back of a radiator in the main hall. It was only then that we

learned that far from being a harmless milk snake, it was in fact a venomous viper!'

"I really think this has to be our Cleo Morris. I mean, I ask you, what are the chances of two different women having such a fascination with snakes? Really?" asked an earnest Mike.

"Good work, Mike, really good work. Tell me, do you know what happened to her after she was excluded from school?" asked Nick.

"A series of boarding schools and a bit of shoplifting, for which she received a couple of cautions. Then it goes quiet for ten years. No trace of her at all. I think it's possible she went abroad."

"Interesting, very interesting." Nick turned to the note-taker.

"Note to myself to raise actions for further enquiries to be made into this Cleo Morris. I want her family members traced and interviewed. We need to establish her identity and current location, we need to find her as soon as possible. Note also for an action to be raised to trace her finger prints which will still be on record."

Mike returned to his seat. Harriet moved her chair closer to him and whispered, "Nick has a new girlfriend, long story, but I saw an enormous tattoo of a snake on her back, it seemed to run the whole length of her body."

"Really? The whole length?"

"Yes!"

"Leave it with me, I'll make some discreet enquiries."

A short break followed, during which Harriet checked her phone. There was a missed call from estate agents Thompson & Timpson. It appeared that a small cottage had just come onto their books; it was in the right area and had recently been modernised. Harriet arranged a viewing for that afternoon.

The briefing resumed, but without Nick, who'd been called away. Derek stepped in and proceedings concluded just before twelve.

As Harriet and Mike stood up to leave Derek called them across. As they entered Nick's office, he closed the door.

"When I spoke to DS Paul Jones this morning, he didn't just provide an update on Alec Brown but also Troy Manning. It seems the tests were delayed as the pathologist was away on holiday. He's back now and the tissue samples do show traces of snake venom."

"Bloody hell," said Mike.

"Yes, but what does it actually mean? It means there is a link between our deceased males and Troy; it means that they all suffered the same death, but what we are no closer to finding out is why," said Harriet.

"That's why we need to find Cleo Morris," said Mike.

"By the way, I haven't told Nick yet." Derek looked solemn.

"Don't just yet, I'm not entirely sure we can trust him. I need to check something out first, as he has a new girlfriend. I'll explain over a pint later," said Mike, exchanging looks with Harriet.

"Okay, I'll hold fire for now, but there is something else I feel I should mention which is kind of linked to how much we tell Nick. After the briefing, I brought Nick's papers back to his office, and a couple of sheets flew off the top. As I picked them up I noticed an email dated today. Your name caught my eye, Harriet, so I read it. It's a warning that you are in danger, it strongly urged Nick to take measures to protect you."

"Really? Who's it from? Can it be trusted?"

"I'm no computer expert but whoever sent it wished to remain anonymous. I'll get it checked out though. Anyway, I wasn't sure what to do, as I'd only seen it by chance. Not knowing if Nick had actioned it, but guessing not, for he didn't have time, I did the only thing I could think of and rang the Chief Constable. Harriet, no objections please, but you are to have twenty-four-hour protection from now on."

"Good," said Mike.

"I'm not going to argue. I'm off to view a cottage this afternoon. If I decide to rent it, I'll let you know immediately," she told them.

"That would be helpful. I can then liaise with the estate agents and get the technical support in to install a security system. Thank you both. Now how about that pint you promised me, Mike?"

The cottage was open plan, light and airy. The front door led into a large double fronted lounge/dining room with a wood burner. The lounge area was carpeted, and the dining area laid with flagstones with a second wood burner. At the back of the cottage was a large farm house Shaker kitchen in duck egg blue, complete with larder and downstairs toilet/utility room and French doors onto a small patio and grass area beyond. At the back of the garden stood a gate onto the escarpment. Upstairs, there was a family bathroom with white suite and a shower, and black and white tiles on walls and floor. There were three bedrooms: one large double at the back with a small shower room and two slightly smaller doubles. Harriet signed a six-month rental agreement that afternoon.

How to tell Nick? She finally decided on a text message; she couldn't face another argument. "*Have found a place to rent in the short-term, hope to move in next week. Would like to take a few items of furniture such as a couple of sofas, a bed, and wardrobe. Will also need some kitchen items, have attached a list. Ring me if you want to discuss. Thanks H.*"

Nick did not respond immediately so Harriet assumed he was fine about it, until that is she received a call on her mobile.

"What the bloody hell do you think you are doing?" he screamed.

"What do you mean?"

"Bloody moving out without discussing it first." Harriet could tell from his tone she would need to tread carefully.

"Wait a minute Nick, I need to find somewhere to live. I can't stay at Mum and Dad's forever."

"And who the fuck's going to pay for it? We have a fucking huge mortgage."

"Nick, please stop swearing, it's just a short-term measure until we sort ourselves out. It's okay, look, you and I need to sit down and talk. It's been crazy lately, but we will find time, I promise."

"You promise, cross your heart?" he sobbed.

"Yes, cross my heart."

"Okay, I'll agree to you renting so long as we have that talk, but you can only take one sofa," he slurred.

"I'm sure that's possible."

"Okay, bye." Nick terminated the call.

Harriet put her head in her hands. She wondered if Nick was on the verge of some sort of breakdown? Frightened for him, she didn't know how to react to a man who had become so unstable and erratic.

There were to be no further outbursts from Nick that week, but mindful of how unbalanced he'd been of late Harriet enlisted Mike and Derek's assistance to load her stuff into a friend's van. Nick was not at home when they arrived, but he had left a note in the kitchen. It wasn't exactly an apology, but it did tell her she was welcome to take as many sofas as she liked.

The house move provided the opportunity for Derek to tell Harriet and Mike about his recent conversations with Chief Constable Mark Jones.

"I thought long and hard about how much to tell him, but in the end, I decided if I was vague, he might not be able to assist. So I outlined the evidence we had in relation to Deputy Chief Constable Jack Peters and DS Steve Smith, which included playing Alec's recording."

"What did he say?" asked Mike.

"Well, something along the lines that the situation was extremely serious. And that on reflection, Jack Peters' behaviour had been troubling of late. He'd taken to making decisions without discussion with the senior management team. He'd also taken to disappearing for long periods and sometimes he failed to show at all. To cut a long story short, he insisted we seek counsel from the Force Solicitor. He advised that we arrest both men, and felt we had sufficient evidence to go for a remand in custody for both."

"This is a step in the right direction," said Mike. Harriet nodded in agreement.

"Did you discuss anything else?" asked Harriet. Derek met her gaze and she lingered a little longer than she meant to, enjoying the moment.

"Well, yes, basically: you two. He was most concerned about you. He asked me to thank you for your loyalty and to tell you that he wholly supports what we are trying to achieve. He agreed with the need for absolute confidence. He is now convinced that the corruption is present at the highest level. It is his view that the fewer people who know the better, until we are sure of our facts and sure of who we can trust. He suspects, however, that the arrest of Jack Peters and Steve Smith will provoke a reaction. He wants us to be very careful, very careful indeed."

Harriet reflected on this and realised that arresting Jack Peters and Steve Smith was paramount to poking a hornets' nest.

Bad news came early the following morning in a call from the hospital. Overnight, Harriet's father had suffered a significant rectal haemorrhage. He'd lost so much blood that a transfusion had been necessary.

"I feel I need to tell you that in the short term, the transfusion will have a positive effect on your father. But, it will only work for a while. In the meantime, however, he has rallied and is awake and sitting up in bed," said the nurse.

Harriet and her mother made for the hospital. George had been moved to a bed on the main ward. He grinned as they entered. The whole time they were there, he did not speak but continued to smile through his overgrown beard. At one point, much to Jane's obvious embarrassment, he blew his nose heartily on the bed sheet, as if it were the most natural thing in the world to do. Harriet had to stifle a giggle.

All too soon the time came for Harriet to head back to the incident room. She leaned forward and tenderly kissed her father on the forehead. As she made her way out, something made her turn to give him one last wave. To her utter delight, he smiled directly at her and put his hand to the side of his head in a salute.

Despite it being mid-August, it was raining hard. Her Protection Officer, Greg, threw her the car keys suggesting she run to the car whilst he went to the pay station. Head down against the pelting rain, Harriet made her way across the tarmac. She became aware of a heavily built lady wearing a grey raincoat approaching.

"Sorry to bother you, but you couldn't change a five-pound note for me, could you? I've not got enough change for the machine," she said.

"I'll have a look." As Harriet delved into her handbag, the woman lunged towards her and forced a cloth in her face.

Greg was not initially concerned, assuming Harriet was in the car in the dry. But when he reached the vehicle, he found there was no trace of her. He found the car keys in a puddle nearby along with her mobile phone.

The driver and passenger were still laughing about the ease with which they'd abducted their backseat passenger when Harriet came around. She felt groggy and it took her several minutes to fully come to. She had no idea how long she'd been unconscious, but it was dark outside. She looked around her. There was a female driving and another in the front passenger seat. She found she couldn't move, her hands and her feet had been tied with electrical cable and she was laid out on the back seat. She listened to the conversation taking place in the front of the car.

"What's in the handbag?" asked the driver.

"Let's see... a makeup bag, tissues, ooh a warrant card, a diary, a purse, nothing much of interest," said the front passenger.

"Look in the diary," said the driver.

"What am I looking for?" replied the passenger.

"Anything of interest."

The passenger fell silent as she went through Harriet's diary. It was soon discarded.

It wasn't long before they turned off the main road and wound their way up a narrow driveway. Harriet could just make out that it was tree-lined. The car swung round and halted on a gravel area. With no idea where she was and undecided on her next move, Harriet pretended to be still under the influence of what she presumed had been chloroform.

It wasn't long before she found herself being lifted from the vehicle and swung over a broad shoulder. Whoever the woman was, she was large framed and very strong. Harriet was carried up several flights of stairs. Eventually, they stopped at a door and entered a cold, musty smelling room. With her hands and feet still bound she was unceremoniously dumped on her back on a small single bed. The door closed, and Harriet was plunged into darkness. A key turned in the lock.

CHAPTER 26

Kate Squires was shown into a non-descript office. Grey metal window frames, grey walls and a grey carpet. There was an emptiness in the pit of her stomach, she bit her nails as she paced up and down. The door opened and a male in a suit entered.

"Kate?" She nodded.

"Well, I've been told by the Chief Constable that I must work with you, that you can be trusted. You will forgive me if I remain cautious for the time being. This is not the way we usually work. Indeed, I don't profess to understand exactly what's going on, but I trust the Chief. It appears that you've been brought in to try to avoid any internal leaks, so you will report directly to me. I'm Derek Wynn."

"I understand. I too find myself in a position I wouldn't have chosen, but I have been directed to work with you and to help you in whatever way I can. And I'm unable to decline to do so."

"Seems we are stuck with each other then." Derek looked at the young woman before him.

"What can you tell me about Jack Peters?" he asked.

"I've learnt that Jack Peters is supremely confident and thoroughly corrupt. His dishonesty is something he wears like a badge of honour. He uses people and does not care who gets hurt in the process. He's a bully who derives personal pleasure from pushing others around. Jack Peters is a vain narcissist, a deeply immoral man."

"You're not a big fan then." Derek was grinning despite himself.

Kate did not reply.

"Well, you are about to meet him in person. You will accompany Superintendent Nick Lacey and myself to his office. Please don't say anything, your role is to observe and take notes of what is said, understood?"

"Yes. Do you want me to record the conversation word for word?"

"If you can, yes please."

As they walked down a long corridor on the top floor of Police Headquarters, Kate could see a man at the far end. He was wearing uniform and sitting at his desk. In fact, he was lounging back in his black leather chair, hands behind his head. As they appeared in the doorway, the man grinned. Kate thought he looked absurdly smug.

"Good morning Nick, good morning Derek. Young lady, how can I help you this lovely morning?" he smirked.

"Can we come in for a minute, Sir?" asked Nick, as Derek closed the door to the office.

"Jack Peters, I'm arresting you for conspiring to assault Detective Sergeant Harriet Lacey, and for participation in the murder of Superintendent Alec Brown. You do not have to say anything, but it may harm your defence if you do not mention, when questioned, something you later rely on in court. Anything you do say may be given in evidence," said Derek.

Kate watched as the smile disappeared. Spots of perspiration appeared on Peters' top lip. For a moment, he said nothing.

"Don't be utterly ridiculous, I'm the Deputy Chief Constable. Have you any idea what you've just accused me of? It's totally outrageous, ridiculous, you can get lost. I absolutely refuse to indulge your foolishness," he bellowed.

"Sir, I'm sorry, but you will need to come with us," said an uncharacteristically calm Nick Lacey.

"Read my lips. I am not going anywhere, now fuck off out of my office before I have you removed. You have no evidence and no idea who you are dealing with," he said with menace.

"Oh, I think they do," said Kate, unable to contain herself. Derek Wynn shot her a look.

"What?" raged Peters.

"I'm sorry, Sir, but you remain under arrest, now please come with us," said Derek.

Remaining seated, Peters reached for his desk phone.

"Sir, can you spare a minute? There has been the most terrible misunderstanding."

Kate watched as Mark Jones, the Chief Constable, emerged from his office opposite and made his way towards them. Jack Peters stood up. "Sir, this is outrageous, Wynn and Lacey are trying to arrest me for some trumped-up fantasy. It's unacceptable, it's contemptible, a disgrace."

"Jack, I fully support Superintendent Lacey and Detective Inspector Wynn. Now I suggest you go quietly or I will ask one of the Police Support Units to come and drag you out. I believe the term is innocent until proven guilty so I suggest you call your solicitor and get him or her working on your behalf. Now, get up and go quietly with these officers," said the Chief firmly.

Jack Peters had no alternative but to do as the Chief Constable instructed, but Kate was sure that he was already planning his revenge.

Mark Jones and Kate were the last to exit the office. "Thank you, Kate, well done. Good to see you again." She smiled back at him.

Kate had just finished writing up her notes when news broke of Harriet's abduction.

CHAPTER 27

Harriet had no idea how long she had been left languishing in the cold, damp, dark room. Indeed, she had no idea whether it was day or night, for the small window behind her head had its shutters tightly closed.

Without warning, a woman entered. With limited visibility Harriet could just make out she was wearing black leather trousers and a grey woollen tunic. The woman moved closer until her face was next to Harriet's, her warm breath caressed Harriet's cheek.

"Good, you're awake."

Someone flicked the light switch and Harriet was able to take a proper look at the woman towering above her. Mid to late twenties, pretty, her long dark hair in a ponytail. Her make-up was subtle, except for her black painted nails. It was Nick's girlfriend, the girl on the stairs. But it was when Harriet spotted a small viper tattoo on the inside of her left wrist that she knew exactly who she was.

"Hello, Cleo." Harriet's heart was racing.

"Well done, Harriet!" sneered Cleo. "I'm impressed."

Harriet didn't reply.

"Now let's get one thing clear from the outset. I'm in charge and you're not. That means I call the shots and you do as I say. Power is a funny thing, Harriet. I have it and you don't. And believe me, if I choose, I can be your worst nightmare. So, let me establish the ground rules. I'm going to ask you some questions and you're going to answer truthfully. If you don't, then you will experience pain the like of which you've never endured before. By the time I've finished with you, you'll be begging me to put you out of your misery, imploring me to finish you off."

Harriet remained silent, wondering how she was going to survive this. It wasn't long before she discovered just how much her silence had annoyed Cleo, who kicked her in the stomach and punched her face. Still tied up, Harriet could do nothing to avoid the blows.

Cleo's mobile chirped into life and she left the room to answer it.

Unable to move and sore, Harriet resolved that no matter what, she would not beg. She was on her own, she knew that, but she would do her utmost to survive, even if her fate had already been sealed.

After a while, Cleo returned. Harriet's feet were untied and she was placed on a chair.

"It's quite simple, Harriet. I just need to know where you've put Troy Manning's note book."

"Troy who? Never heard of him." For this she received another kick in the stomach and punch to the face.

"Troy Manning's note book, where is it?"

Harriet remained silent.

Time and again Cleo tried, but, Harriet remained steadfast, claiming that she didn't know what Cleo was talking about. The more she denied knowledge, the harder and more frequently she was hit, until eventually she lost consciousness.

Sometime later Harriet awoke. Her whole body hurt. She could feel her face was swollen, particularly her lip and her right eye. Her stomach felt like it had been run over by a very large truck.

There was to be no respite. Every two hours for two or three days, Harriet wasn't sure exactly how long, Cleo would appear. Sometimes it was ice cold water thrown over her as she slept. Sometimes fists. Sometimes props were used to beat her. Between the assaults, Harriet explored her tiny sparsely furnished room, looking for a way out. Try as she might, she was unable to prise open the shuttered windows. The door was solid, the floorboards nailed down. It was hopeless. Exhausted, she wasn't sure how much more she could take. Her situation was bleak for she was sure no-one knew where she was. It could only be a matter of time before Cleo lost it and killed her.

The next time Cleo appeared, she brought a companion with her: a huge python draped around her neck. She made a fuss of it, kissing and caressing the gigantic serpent. To Harriet, it was grotesque. It was as much as she could do not to be sick. It took every ounce of her remaining strength not to show her revulsion. In her terror, she began to perspire. She knew Cleo would be watching for any sign of weakness she could exploit. She prayed Cleo would not notice the beads of sweat forming on her top lip. So anxious was she that her breathing became shallow and she became dizzy. When she regained consciousness, the snake had gone. Cleo was standing over her observing her closely, before setting to work on her again. This time she abandoned the kicking and punching for a cigarette lighter. Still, Harriet held out.

"You really are the most stubborn fucking bitch I have ever encountered," Cleo growled. "Just tell me where the diary is and this will all be over." She was burning the flesh on Harriet's forearm as she spoke. Harriet had reached her tipping point.

"Which bit of I don't know what the bloody hell you are talking about don't you understand? You stupid cow, are you thick or something?" she screamed.

Cleo stared back, mouth open, before she lunged forward and punched Harriet in the face.

"That was predictable, Cleo. You can do better than that," taunted Harriet.

Cleo looked at her prey quizzically for a moment. Would she ever tire of the violence? wondered Harriet.

"You know, the death of your friend Professor Hudson was pointless. He really was a foolish man not to talk to me. I mean, it's strange, you seem to evoke such emotion in men: some aspire to protect you, others to silence you. You must be very special, except, it would appear, to your husband. You know he's quite the lover."

Colouring, Harriet flung herself from her chair, striking Cleo with such force that she was knocked to the ground.

"You fucking bitch."

Harriet landed heavily on the floorboards. It took her a few moments to get to her feet. Meanwhile Cleo had turned white and seemed to be struggling to breathe. Her face was etched with pain.

"What's the matter, Cleo? Can't take your own medicine?"

With no reply forthcoming, Harriet continued her rant.

"You know, I don't get you. You are pretty, well educated, clearly intelligent, and yet you choose to do the bidding of others. Well, that's what you do, isn't it? You're someone else's bitch. You follow their orders. You pretend, but you're not running the show; someone else is pulling your strings. Is it just that you are not up to it? Scared you'll fail?" Harriet was expecting a blow to the head any minute, but it didn't come.

Still looking pained and breathless, Cleo clambered to her feet.

"Harriet, Harriet, this isn't personal you know. You've failed to include one very important fact. You have no option but to follow orders. I choose to, for now. You do know I'm going to kill you, don't you? Usually I feel nothing towards my victims, it's a job, but in a peculiar way, you remind me of myself."

"Oh, my God, I can't wait to hear your rationale for that!" said Harriet sarcastically.

"You may mock, but we're really not that different. We're both loners, we don't seek close female friends, we're self-assured, self-reliant and very good at what we do. We're thorough, possess enquiring minds, are intelligent and have a clear sense of self-worth."

208

"We do?"

"Yes, we do. We're capable, strong, and we don't suffer fools gladly. You know, in another life, we would be friends."

"Cleo, I can assure you that would never happen. You're missing one vital factor here, we sit on opposing ends of the moral compass."

Cleo laughed loudly. "A minor detail."

"But that's just it, it's not minor, it's fundamental to everything we do. It's what drives us. How do you do what you do? How do you justify the pain and misery you leave in your wake?"

"I don't, it's a job." And she left the room.

Harriet dropped to the floor and sobbed, for her father, for her marriage, for Poppy, for Andrew Hudson, and out of sheer exhaustion and pain.

Cleo did not visit for a day or two, but the cold and damp were miserable. By now Harriet was in desperate need of a shower. She kept herself busy drawing on the walls with a small pencil she'd found underneath the bed, concentrating on images that made her happy: birds, animals, friends and family. It helped to keep her mind off the pain and hunger. During this period a wisp of a girl in her late teens began to visit. She brought facial wipes, a deodorant, a change of clothes, a bottle of water and a sandwich. The girl didn't say a word, just put the items on the bed. Despite her best efforts, Harriet could not persuade the girl to speak. She wasn't very tall, of slight build painfully thin with greasy mousy shoulder length hair and delicate fragile-looking features. She never stayed more than a couple of minutes at a time. Most welcome of all was the blanket she left on her third visit.

During the long lonely hours, Harriet had plenty of time to reflect amongst the squalor and pain. Sitting on the floor in the dark she began to think about the day she'd been removed from Operation Eagle. She recalled she'd been entering and labelling paperwork from Troy Manning's house. Then it started to come back to her, there'd been a smoke damaged orange exercise book containing number sequences.

"That must be it," she said out loud.

How clever, to hide a directory of your most important and influential clients disguised as lists of numbers in a mundane looking note book. But why hadn't they been found amongst the exhibits?

Harriet closed her eyes. E61715, that was it, the exhibit number! A short while later she decided to leave a message for Derek and Mike, believing that she would likely be dead by the time they found her. She scribbled on the wall.

Harriet had now been incarcerated in the tiny damp room for more days than she could recall. That evening the young girl appeared with a sandwich and another bottle of water. There was no plan, but as the girl placed the items on the bed Harriet leapt on the girl's back, jabbing the pencil in her hand into the girl's neck. The girl cried out in pain and crumpled into a heap on the bed, knocked off balance by the speed of the attack. Deftly, Harriet tied the girl to the bedstead with the electrical cable that had been used to tie her. Half way through, Harriet paused to listen; silence, no-one had heard. She tore a strip of bed sheet off and used it to gag the young girl, whose large tear-filled eyes looked entreatingly back.

"I'm so, so, sorry, you've been nothing but kind to me. I hope I haven't hurt you too much? But I had no other choice, death is all that is left for me here." To her utter surprise the girl nodded in apparent agreement.

Cautiously, Harriet left the room. She found herself in a long corridor with no carpets, just floor boards. Her whole body was shaking. She could hear female laughter below. Not willing to risk the main staircase she explored the other end of the landing instead. To her relief, there was a small staircase at the far end. Probably the old servants' stairs. Thinking that the narrow staircase might lead down to an old scullery or kitchen, she took off her pumps and tip-toed her way down, eventually reaching a hallway just off the old kitchen. The flag-stones were cold underfoot.

At the end of the hallway was a door to the outside. Listening intently for any sign of movement, she made a dash for the door. Cautiously she turned the handle, but the door would not budge. She tried again, with mounting alarm. Unable to locate a key, she began to panic. Entering the scullery, she tried each window in turn but they would not budge, they seemed to be painted shut. With a mounting sense of doom she moved into the old kitchen, but found the same problem. She was about to give up when she spotted a sash window behind the sink. Leaning across she took hold of the brass handles and yanked them with all the strength she could muster. To her utter relief, the window slowly began to edge open, but it was stiff. Climbing into the sink, she gave the window another yank. It opened sufficiently to allow her to squeeze through and drop to the ground.

The air was cold, it made her catch her breath. Carefully, she felt her way around the back of the house towards the front lawn area, only to hear voices approaching. Breathless, she froze. Unsure what to do she looked around her for somewhere to hide. She saw an old coal bunker to her left and just managed to dart behind it as two female guards with Doberman dogs walked past. She held her breath; she could hear radio chatter which meant there were others on site. Her plan to simply walk out of this nightmare was shattered.

Fearing the dogs might detect her scent she retraced her steps before setting off in the opposite direction towards an old stable block. Finding the stables had been converted into garages, she looked for somewhere to conceal herself. There was a pile of old tarpaulin on the floor. She crawled under an old Land Rover Defender, and pulled the tarpaulin over her.

CHAPTER 28

Dawn broke. Cold and stiff, Harriet rubbed her eyes. Bloodied and bruised, her whole body was tender. Just for the moment, her natural optimism left her. She wasn't sure if she could be bothered to move. Somehow, she knew she had to muster the energy, but the Doberman dogs were a real problem, and she guessed that by now her flight had been discovered.

Raised voices and barking dogs brought her back to consciousness. She listened intently; the disturbance seemed to be coming from the front of the house. Weak and exhausted, she dragged herself to her feet and made her way towards the fracas, using the walls of the old stable yard to steady her. It was a cold September morning. She shivered, for she wasn't dressed for such conditions. Her thin cotton leggings and baggy tunic failed to keep the cold breeze from penetrating her battered body. It took her some time to negotiate her way around the kitchen garden to a corner section, where she found a small gap to peer through.

On the driveway were several individuals. Harriet could see security uniforms and Dobermans. As she looked more closely she counted four females being restrained by guards. Dressed in camouflage gear, they didn't look dissimilar to the covert police teams Harriet was familiar with. Although they fought to break free, they were overwhelmed.

Further away, Harriet spotted another group of security staff marching a single female towards the others. Although not close enough to hear what was being said she saw the situation escalate as one of the captive women was struck in the face and another kicked in the stomach. Then she spotted Cleo and her heart sank, for she knew this was as serious as it could get and there would certainly be casualties.

The mere sight of Cleo made Harriet shudder. She was now quite sure she was a psychopath. Harriet sensed she was unlikely to survive another encounter with her.

Cautiously, she edged her way around the side of the walled vegetable garden to find a better vantage point. The garden had clearly been spectacular in its day. As she walked, she passed the remains of large glass greenhouses, a stone-built dove cote, bee-keeping equipment and, most amazing of all, a pineapple hothouse.

As Harriet reached her new position, she could see Cleo clearly. She was little more than a metre away and appeared to be deep in conversation with a tall, athletic, beautiful young woman. Indeed, the two women could have been sisters, so similar were they. The second woman, however, had a grace, a presence, that Cleo lacked and, despite the seriousness of the situation, appeared calm. It struck Harriet that she looked remarkably like the woman on the CCTV footage from the hotel in Sheffield. Despite everything, Harriet was intrigued.

Edging slightly closer, she strained to hear the conversation taking place on the lawn of what had undoubtedly been an impressive and elegant country residence in its day. She surveyed the sweeping drive that had once welcomed aristocratic horse-drawn carriages, now unkempt and overgrown with weeds. The outline of the formal gardens was just discernible above the overgrowth. And there was just the hint of terracing.

"What have you done with her, Cleo?"

"Why the interest, Kate?"

"You know better than to ask me that," came the curt response.

"You're right, I do, but there is no way that I am handing her over without an explanation, and even then I'm unlikely to."

"We'll see about that."

"Well, I'd hardly say you're able to bargain. What were you thinking? You amateur. You've no idea how much I will enjoy extracting the truth from your friends over there." And with that she shouted across.

"Are they talking yet?"

Harriet could see two or three heads shaking in response.

"Try pulling their teeth out one by one. Get some pliers and pull out all their teeth." She swung around. Harriet ducked, remaining unnoticed for now.

"For God's sake Cleo, please don't!" shouted Kate. "This is absolute madness, leave them alone, they're young. If you need someone to take it out on then that would be me."

The sickening sound of high pitched shrieking started to drift across the lawn.

"Cleo, stop, please stop. It's barbaric!"

"You should have thought of that before you embarked on this ridiculous rescue mission. I won't give her up. Now tell me why you really want her?"

"I can't."

"You mean you won't. Has it got something to do with that secret organisation you belong to?"

"Stop playing games, Cleo, and let them go, please."

"No, I don't think I will."

"Let them go and let her go. You can have me."

"Tempting, but no I don't think so, unless you want to tell me about your secret society?"

Harriet didn't understand what was going on. It was surreal. Torture? Really? What the hell was she mixed up in? And, who were they talking about, who did they both want so badly?

"Look, I'm not leaving without Harriet Lacey. I will rescue her, or I'll die trying."

"How melodramatic, Kate, but you're not having her. Really, why would you risk yourself for a meddling copper? She has spirit, I'll grant you, but she's such a stubborn bitch. Tell me why you want her so much?"

"Cleo, if I thought you were capable of understanding I might consider it, but you are so focussed on yourself you can't see the bigger picture." And with that Kate swung at Cleo, striking her hard in the face and knocking her to the ground.

Harriet stood motionless, heart pounding. It had never occurred to her that she was the topic of the overheard conversation. What should she do now? She hesitated. Whatever the reason Kate wanted her, it surely had to be better than the prospect of being re-captured by Cleo? In any case, she couldn't sit by, even in her sorry state, and watch those young women suffer any further.

As fast as her poor body would allow, she limped back to the old stable block to the dilapidated Land Rover Defender. With no real experience of hot-wiring cars, she was relieved to find the keys in the ignition. As she clambered into the driver's seat she turned the key and the vehicle burst into life. Revving the engine, she put the car into reverse and floored the accelerator. The car shot out of the garage.

Harriet made straight for Cleo and Kate, who were still fighting. The sight of the approaching vehicle was enough to separate them. Harriet drove straight at Cleo, only turning at the last minute, but not before clipping her left side. Cleo howled as she collapsed. Selecting reverse, Harriet sped back, skidding on the wet grass before pulling alongside Kate.

"Get in!" Harriet screamed. Kate quickly obliged. As they sped across the lawn, Harriet noticed Kate was staring at her. Glancing at her forearms she saw they were covered in burn marks, her wrists bruised and welted. She used her tongue to explore her cut and swollen lip. The rear-view mirror revealed bruising around her eyes.

"I'm guessing from the look on your face, I look a bit of a state," she said.

"I can't begin to imagine what you've been through. Did Cleo do this to you?" Kate looked horrified.

"We can talk later, but for now I need your help to identify your friends. I'll do my best to get the others out of the way."

And that's exactly what she did. Backwards and forwards across the lawn, using the vehicle to scatter the opposition. Harriet tried her best not to leave life-changing injuries but it was hard to be accurate. It wasn't long before the opposition retreated to the house, possibly to re-group. This gave Kate the opportunity to round up her team and call for help. But it did not prove long enough for them to escape.

A white Range Rover appeared. Immediately Harriet spotted it, she knew it was Cleo. Her heart sank. Now there would be no avoiding a final encounter. She did not feel panic, just regret and a sudden rush of sadness that she wouldn't see her children again. There was no time to dwell, for the Range Rover was bearing down on her at speed. Harriet knew she could not out-run it, it was a far more powerful vehicle. Her only option was to use the Defender as a kind of battering ram.

"Run to the tree line over there and wait," she shouted to Kate.

"Harriet, this is suicide, you have no hope of success, you will die!" Kate had tears in her eyes.

"Then so be it. I can't stand by and watch. I must do something and whilst I am alive, Cleo is more interested in me than you. So, please go!"

Before Kate could reply, Harriet had driven off. She spun the Defender to face the fast-moving Range Rover, but at the last minute she turned the wheel sharply to the left, resulting in a noisy impact with Cleo's front right wing. To her surprise, the Defender appeared to suffer less damage than the Range Rover. Time and again the two women pitted their vehicles against each other, but each impact caused further damage to Harriet's already weak and injured body.

Cleo drove like a woman possessed, her anger exhibited in her erratic and dangerous manoeuvres. It was clear she no longer cared about her beautiful car, she was intent on destroying Harriet. Harriet realised she would have to find a way to get an advantage, if she were to stand any chance of surviving. Then she saw her opportunity, she would lure Cleo over the edge of the lawn to the terrace below. Cleo made straight for her.

Carefully, Harriet controlled the Defender over the top terrace to the lower lawn. As Cleo came racing after her it was blatantly clear she hadn't seen that the edge of the top lawn fell away. Harriet put her foot down hard on the accelerator to ensure she wasn't caught and just before reaching the next stone edged terrace slammed the Defender hard to the left, just out of Cleo's reach. The Range Rover flew past, clipping the stone edge, and was catapulted through the air, landing heavily on its roof in a shallow pond beneath. But in Harriet's efforts to avoid Cleo she'd inadvertently put the Defender on a collision path with a large grassy bank. There was no avoiding it and, despite desperate attempts to brake, the vehicle hit the bank at speed, throwing Harriet forward.

Her head hit the windscreen with such force the glass cracked.

Harriet struggled to catch her breath. Her chest felt tight, her forehead throbbed. She grappled to undo her seatbelt. There was only one thing on her mind: Cleo. As she got out of the vehicle her legs gave way beneath her. She got back to her feet and started to make for the edge of the terrace. She had to see for herself.

"Where are you going?" Kate shouted after her.

"To find Cleo."

"Harriet, you're injured, you need treatment. Leave Cleo. I'll look."

"No, I need to see for myself."

Kate sprinted to catch up. Taking Harriet by the hand she helped her over the edge of the terrace and down the steep slope. The upturned Range Rover lay in a crumpled heap. Forcing their way through the undergrowth, they went to the driver's side. They could see Cleo still in the driving seat, but she was upside down and unconscious. Although she had sustained serious facial injuries, she did appear to be breathing.

The vehicle was locked. Harriet picked up a large rock and began to strike the side window, over and over, but to no avail.

"Harriet, the glass is toughened, you're not going to get in that way," said Kate.

"But I need to try."

"Why do you? Why? After everything she's done to you,

after all the pain, all the fear? Why do you need to do anything?"

"Because '*The greatness of humanity is not in being human, but in being humane*'."

"Says who?" asked Kate.

"Mahatma Gandhi."

In that moment the helicopter arrived, and Kate began to pace, concerned that Cleo's followers might re-appear at any moment. She looked across at Harriet, who was slumped against the upturned vehicle, rasping for breath.

"Time to go, Harriet," said Kate decisively. With the help of some of the others, they carried her to the helicopter. As it took off, Harriet lost consciousness.

CHAPTER 29

When the helicopter was airborne, Kate made a call.

"Dad."

"I'm putting you on speaker phone, Cyrus is with me. Are you okay?"

"I am, but Harriet's very poorly."

"What's her condition?" asked Cyrus.

"She's seriously injured and has deteriorated since we became airborne. She's in and out of consciousness. It all went wrong at the house and it was she who rescued us. How she found the courage to face Cleo again I'll never know, for she suffered terribly at her hand."

"What do you mean?" asked Kate's father.

"Oh, Dad, she's covered in bruises and cuts. I saw a black eye, a cut above her eyebrow, bruising on her jaw, a cut and swollen lip, burn marks on her arms, bruising from ties on her wrists and ankles, and she was limping terribly."

"That's truly awful. Where is Cleo now?" asked Cyrus.

"Unconscious and upside down in her Range Rover, which is on its roof in a pond. I've called the emergency services."

"Well done, we need to think about our next move very carefully," said Kate's father.

"I feel awful. I misjudged Cleo and, in my haste to act, I

put everyone at risk. If it hadn't been for Harriet, I don't know what would have happened. As it is, some of my team have lost teeth, pulled out with pliers on Cleo's orders." Kate's voice cracked.

"You handled yourself extremely well," said Kate's father.

"Cleo is incredibly dangerous, and I know for a fact you undertook due diligence on this job. It's unfortunate that some of the intelligence was out of date. You were right to go in when you did. Due to her new collaboration, Cleo has access to greater resources. The electrification of the perimeter fence and pressure pads around the gates are all brand new. They weren't there last week. So pick yourself up, it's not always possible to plan for every eventuality. But you got everyone out alive. We will find a way to sort this mess out," said Cyrus kindly.

"The priority now is to get Harriet medical assistance," said Kate's Dad.

"I don't believe we have any choice now but to work more closely with the police. Kate, I want you to contact Derek Wynn and arrange to see him. Don't worry, I will come with you on the car journey to brief you. From now on you will need to help them to unravel this case and bring those responsible to justice. Derek Wynn is a good man, a man you can trust. It may not be comfortable for you at times, but it will be alright, I promise," said Cyrus.

"Okay, but what about Nick Lacey?"

"He's disappeared, it's quite the mystery," said Kate's father.

Kate's head was spinning, she wasn't sure what Cyrus was asking of her. Was he hinting that she would have to own up to her presence at the scene of Professor Grey's death? And her intervention at the university? But she trusted Cyrus, so would be guided by him. She made the call.

"Derek, it's Kate Squires. Can I come and see you? It's urgent."

"Yes, I'm in my office. Is everything okay?"

"Yes and no. Do you mind if I fill you in when I get there? I'll be about forty minutes."

"That's fine. See you then."

When Kate arrived, she found a subdued Derek sitting at his desk, surrounded by piles of papers.

"Hi Kate, good to see you again, come in." Derek stood up and offered his hand.

"Thank you, and you. What are you up to?"

"I'm sitting here feeling sorry for myself, hoping against hope that Harriet is still alive."

"Derek..."

"I know she's strong and resourceful, but... I can't get her out of my mind; it's been a very long time since I've had such strong feelings for anyone."

"Derek..."

"I feel lost without her around. I just want to see her again."

"Derek..."

"I feel helpless. For possibly the first time in my life, I'm at a loss as to what to do next."

"Derek, listen, will you, please."

"I keep having the same nightmare over and over..."

"Derek!" shouted Kate. "Harriet is alive."

"She is? She is?" he said jumping to his feet.

"Yes."

"Oh, thank God, but how do you know and is she okay?"

"Because I was with her. It's a long story, she's injured and needs urgent medical attention."

"Will she be alright? What are her injuries? Can I see her?"

"Yes, I sincerely hope she will. I don't know the full extent of her injuries and please don't go off the deep end but she's been flown out of the country for her own safety. Please trust me when I say she is receiving the best possible care, but it's just not safe for her here."

"Really? What's been going on?"

"It's a long and complicated story, but the UK is unsafe for her right now."

"I've so many questions... Where was she? Who had her?"

"We found her at a place called Highfield Hall in Surrey. Cleo had her."

"Oh, my god. Cleo Morris?"

Kate nodded.

"Did she hurt her?"

"I'm afraid she suffered terribly at Cleo's hands."

Before Derek could ask any more, his phone sounded.

"I see... yes, Sir ... yes, I understand... no Sir, it's not a problem... yes, thank you."

"Is everything alright?"

"Yes, it seems we are to work together once more. That was the Chief Constable. I understand that not only will you be able to provide a different perspective to this investigation, but you may be able to help us to move it forward. Welcome to the team."

"Thank you. I promise I will do everything in my power to help."

"I believe you. Now I need to get my head together and decide on a plan, but before I do, I must ask: do you know the whereabouts of Cleo Morris?"

"When we left she was unconscious and trapped in her Range Rover, on the Highfield Estate. I called the emergency services, but you may wish to ensure she doesn't slip away."

"Exactly."

Kate listened while Derek contacted Surrey Police. He spoke to a Superintendent Channing. It appeared Cleo was still trapped in her vehicle. The two Senior Officers arranged to meet at the scene later that afternoon.

As Derek put the phone down a man with long sideburns, wearing a crumpled grey suit, sidled into the office.

"Mike, I'd like you to meet Kate Squires, she's going to be helping us with our enquiries." Derek winked at Kate.

"What the fuck?"

Kate stepped forward and held out her hand. Mike hesitated for a moment before taking it.

"Mike, its fine, it's been sanctioned by the Chief Constable."

"Okay," said Mike slowly, but Kate didn't think he sounded too convinced.

"More importantly she's brought fantastic news. Harriet's alive."

"Really? Oh, thank God. Is she okay? When can I see her?"

"She's injured but receiving treatment and being kept safe. It may be a while until she is well enough to be seen, but Kate will ensure she's well looked after."

It didn't take Derek and Mike long to assemble a small team of detectives and Scenes of Crime Officers, including Harriet's admirer DS Paul Jones. Kate was not keen on returning to Surrey but remained silent. Within a couple of hours they were on the road. They arrived just in time to see the badly injured occupant of a white Range Rover being placed on a stretcher. Paramedics had fought hard to stabilise her, but Cleo remained in a critical condition.

While Derek went in search of Superintendent Channing, the rest of the team made their way into the hallway of the big house to wait for him. A short time later they climbed the imposing main staircase towards the attic rooms. As they ascended Kate was struck by the vastness of the house. Enormous landings to the left and right, lofty ceilings, intricate plaster stucco. Having said that, considerable portions of the house were dilapidated. Gaping holes in the roof had caused significant water damage.

The smallest of the old servants' quarters was tucked in a corner of the topmost hallway. Three steps led to a solid wooden door; there were various bolts on the outside and a large key in the metal lock. They entered the grim little room.

Paul Jones set to work. Less than an hour later he called out to the others.

"Well, I can confirm she was kept in this room. I now need to work out what happened in here." Further investigation revealed traces of Harriet's blood all over the room.

Mike had been studying Harriet's graffiti wall.

"Boss, come and look at this." He beckoned Derek across. Mike was pointing to an image on the wall. Derek took out his glasses to examine it closer. From where she was standing Kate could see it was a letter and five numbers, encircled by some sort of bird.

"What do you think this means?" Derek was scrutinising the wall.

"I'm not entirely sure." Mike pulled a face. He appeared to be thinking.

"You beauty!" he suddenly shouted. Taking his mobile from his pocket, he made a call.

"Trevor, its Mike. I need a quick favour. Can you access the HOLMES database for operation Eagle and put in the following number E61715, then ring me back and tell me what it is?"

Everyone in the room stopped what they were doing and waited expectantly for Mike's mobile to ring. It didn't take long.

"Mike. Trev. It's an orange exercise book containing

numerous handwritten number sequences. It was found amongst Troy Manning's papers, but it's missing from the store."

"Missing, you say? Who booked it onto the HOLMES system?"

"That would have been Detective Sergeant Harriet Lacey."

"Okay, thanks so much, mate."

Mike turned to the others. "I think Harriet left us a message. I took a guess that the E on the wall stood for Eagle, but to help me, she had helpfully drawn one. Trev has just confirmed that this number relates to an exhibit, an orange note book belonging to Troy Manning. Why would a notepad of numbers have caused such a stir? Unless the numbers are code? What if the book contains the names of his high-profile clients? It seems it's missing from the exhibits store. It was Harriet who processed it, put it onto the system."

"Well done, Mike." Derek walked across and patted him on the back. "We now know thanks to Steve Smith's change of heart that Jack Peters and his cronies were desperate to get their hands on it. It would make sense that they also knew Harriet was the last to handle it and they wanted to ensure its destruction. After everything that's happened it seems logical that they went after Harriet when they couldn't locate it in the evidence store."

Mike walked across to Kate. "Can we speak to Harriet on the phone? We've made what we think is a fucking crucial discovery."

"I'm really sorry Mike, but the latest is that she's stable but still unconscious."

As the room fell silent Superintendent Dave Channing popped his head around the door.

"Derek and team, we've found something I think you might want to see. In all my years as an officer, I've never seen anything like it."

Intrigued, they downed tools. In the middle of the house they came across a solid metal door with keypad access. As they entered the state of the art laboratory, it was immediately obvious why this room had generated such interest. There were more than fifty glass tanks, and each tank housed at least one live snake.

"Oh, my God." Mike shuddered. "We need a fucking snake expert."

"Already onto it," said Supt Channing breezily. "We should have one arriving in the next half an hour."

Within the hour, reptile expert Dr Gina Wood appeared. A slightly plump, middle-aged lady with a severe auburn bob, wearing thick-rimmed glasses, bright red lipstick and a long flowing red skirt.

"Good afternoon one and all," she boomed. "I know you're incredibly busy, so I'll try to keep this as brief as possible. What we have here is undoubtedly a snake farm, there's evidence of quite a black mamba breeding programme."

A stir went around the room.

"The black mamba is the largest venomous snake in Africa; it usually grows to between 8.2 and 10ft in length and is thought to be the fastest snake in the world. Commonly brown, grey or khaki on its back. It's the ink-black colouration of the inside of its mouth that gives it its name. The genus and species name is derived from the Ancient Greek words *Dendroapis* meaning 'tree asp' and *Polylepis* meaning 'many scaled'. Its bite is often referred to as 'The kiss of death'. Before anti-venom, death was certain. It has the most rapid acting venom of any snake species and can kill a person within thirty minutes."

"Looks like we've found the source of the venom then," Mike whispered to Derek.

"Yes, indeed."

After supper, Mike and Kate went in search of Derek. They found him nursing a whisky in a corner of the bar lounge at their hotel.

"What are you up to?" asked Kate.

"Well, I've been sitting here trying to link things together. I'm convinced that many of the events of the last few weeks are connected. But right now I'm struggling to see the bigger picture."

"Would you like some help?" asked Mike.

"Yes, that would be great. Grab yourselves a drink; I've got a tab, room twenty-five..." He waited until the two had returned before continuing.

"Right then, let's start with the discovery of a female's mutilated body, near Tower Bridge. It turns out the victim was an informant of DC Rebecca Wood from Operation Eagle. Rebecca is an experienced detective. The official line is that she failed to register her informant, but I don't believe that. There will be an enquiry and Rebecca's future in the police hangs in the balance."

"This all sounds like a bit of a smoke screen to me. I think it's far more likely that the informant hit a nerve. I'm happy to look at this, if you'd like?" said Mike.

"Have you got the time? You'll need to tread carefully," said Derek.

"Yes."

"What else has happened?" asked Kate.

"Nick Lacey disappeared, which occurred within a week of Harriet's abduction. It remains a mystery: his phone, his wallet, and his passport were all found on the kitchen table. His car, in a station car park about twenty miles away. There have been no sightings of him and his bank account hasn't been touched. It feels like a suicide, but there is no note and no body." Derek got to his feet and stretched before continuing.

"CCTV footage from the back yard shows him turning left onto the high street, and heading in the direction of the north of the town. We picked him up again in Windsor Street, then Alexander Avenue, but after that nothing. Alexander Avenue is not far from his home address. Best guess is that he went home briefly, before driving to the train station and leaving his car. The CCTV at the station shows him parking the car at five forty-five p.m. After that he disappears. There is no evidence that he caught a train."

"I see," said Kate. She had decided in that moment not to

reveal that she already knew about Nick. It would just lead to awkward questions.

"Nick and I were in my office reviewing CCTV footage of Jack's death, when Nick made his excuses and left, he never returned," said Derek.

"Jack Peters is dead?" exclaimed Kate.

"Yes, I'll talk about that in more detail in a minute," said Derek.

"I'm sure you've already thought of this but is it possible Nick saw something on the Cell footage that caused him to take flight?" asked Kate.

"No, that didn't cross my mind, I thought it had to be something to do with the conversation we'd been having about Harriet's disappearance. As soon as we get back to the station that CCTV footage will be a priority. Good thinking Kate."

"It's been my experience that most of what you need to know is usually hidden from view on phones and laptops. Have you looked at them?"

"I wasn't aware he had a laptop. I don't recall seeing one and we certainly didn't find one at his address, nor in his office," said Derek.

"I'd be stunned if there isn't one somewhere. What about his phone? What did that yield?"

"Nothing of note, but I will ask them back at Chapel to make a concerted effort to find his laptop. Let's move on for now."

Kate hesitated. She was unsure whether now was a good

time to offer her assistance with any laptop that might come to light. She decided it could wait.

"Then we have the murder of Jack Peters in the holding cells of the Magistrates Court." Derek looked straight at Kate.

"It has to be linked. I'd be really interested in seeing the footage. Does it show the moment he was killed?" asked Kate.

"It's not obvious how he died, to be honest. We'd only just started to look at it when Nick disappeared. It's a priority to get back to it though." Derek drained his glass.

CHAPTER 30

Kate could not fault the way she was being treated. Derek Wynn and Mike Taylor were nothing but open, there'd been no hint of mistrust. Though still uneasy in her new role, she had to admit that she was beginning to enjoy the challenge.

Next morning Kate, Mike and Derek drove back to the incident room, arriving late morning. That afternoon, Mike burst into Derek's office with Kate in tow.

"Afternoon, boss; do me a favour and ask Kate what she does for a living." Mike was grinning.

"So, Kate, what do you do for a living?"

Laughing, she replied, "I run a small computer network security company with a friend. I think this might be Nick Lacey's laptop." She handed it to Derek.

"Really? How come?"

"Because it transpires it was Nick Lacey who first showed you the CCTV. He brought the laptop to your office. Mike later picked it up assuming it was yours."

"And you know that how?" asked Derek.

"I took the liberty of taking a quick look."

"And?" Derek was on the edge of his seat.

"There are numerous recently deleted files. With your permission, my team would be happy to look at restoring these."

"I'd appreciate that, thank you, it would be especially useful as we still don't know who we can trust."

"So, there's a good chance that we could soon have actions coming out of this?" asked Mike.

"Based on previous experience, I'd say there is a very good chance that its contents will prove illuminating," said Kate.

"Good work, both of you. Now let's have another look at the CCTV." Derek opened the laptop.

The footage clearly showed Jack Peters being returned to his cell following the remand application. Flanked by two security personnel, a male and a female, he could be seen resisting re-entry to the cell. As the male blocked the doorway, the female officer took Jack's arm. She could be seen saying something in his ear. At first Jack looked relieved but then his facial expression changed. Derek froze the image.

"Does anyone else think the guard looks hateful?" said Kate.

"She certainly doesn't look too friendly." Mike put his glasses on and took a closer look at the screen.

"I'd go further, there's almost a malicious look to her." Derek pressed play again.

The guard seemed to be trying to steady Peters; she placed her arm around his upper body and lowered him into a sitting position on the cell bench.

"Look at Peters' face." Kate pointed to the screen.

Derek rewound the footage. Peters was leaning against the wall; all colour had drained from his face, he was motionless. Replaying the footage over and over, they could not get a clear view of the female guard. Kate was about to give up when she spotted something.

"There, look! Left wrist, just peeping out from under the glove."

"Oh my God." Derek paused the screen.

"Bloody hell." Mike jumped to his feet.

"Is that Cleo Morris?" said a wide-eyed Derek.

"You know, I think it is. She must have had inside help," said Kate.

"What do you mean?" Mike looked confused.

"Well, I happen to know she was recently head-hunted, resulting in access to greater resources and connections."

"So, she accompanies Jack from the police station into the court, and then following the remand hearing murders him in his cell. Hang on a minute, look at this bit of footage. I think they may have known each other," said Mike excitedly.

"Oh yes, they know each other. Jack Peters put work Cleo's way but they recently had a falling out and Cleo is now working for Peters' boss."

"Are you sure?" asked Derek.

"Yes."

"Can you say how you know?"

"I could, but I'm not sure you'd be so happy about it."

"So, you wouldn't be able to make a statement?"

"No."

"Really?"

Kate shook her head vigorously.

"Okay, I'm not going to push you now. But we will have to re-visit this."

"Can we see if the footage shows Cleo's lips moving? If it does I have an idea," said Mike.

They looked at the footage again, and it did indeed show Cleo talking to Peters.

"Wait a minute." Mike left the room, returning less than five minutes later with a member of support staff.

"Sally can read lips. I know it's not very scientific, but if it's relevant we can always get it verified. I want to know what Cleo says to Peters," said Mike, turning to Sally.

"Me too," said Wynn, suddenly looking reinvigorated by the turn of events.

They all crowded around the screen.

"Hi Jack, bet I'm the last person you expected to see? This isn't personal, just business. It was lucrative working for you, but your boss is so much more generous. Sleep tight, Jack."

"This is immense; I can't believe she's so brazen," said Mike, breaking the silence.

"That's Cleo all over: bare-faced, greedy, clever and deadly," said Kate.

"You know her personally?" asked Derek.

"I had the misfortune to be at the same boarding school for a while. She made my life a misery. It didn't help that our mothers had an intense dislike for each other. It's complicated."

"Bloody sounds it," said Mike.

"Have you had dealings with her other than at Highfield Hall?" asked Derek, looking directly into her green eyes.

"Yes."

"Care to elaborate?"

"If I must?"

Derek nodded.

"I first came across her by chance in early spring when she brought her laptop in for repair and an upgrade. She didn't see me, but I personally carried out the work."

"And you saw something that made you suspicious?" said Mike.

"Something like that."

"And?" said Derek.

"And there were several occasions when our paths crossed in one way or another," said Kate, sighing.

"And there was a bloody good reason why you didn't contact the police with your suspicions?" asked Derek.

"There was."

"Okay, that's enough for now. Let's see if we can work out how Cleo disposed of Jack," said Derek.

"I'm guessing she stuck to her usual M.O. but she was subtle about it. It's possible she was able to inject him when she put her arm across to steady him. Look, she leans over him and pauses," said Kate.

"Yep, seems the most obvious explanation, but why kill him?" said Mike.

"I think you might find that Peters had become a liability, a loose cannon," said Kate.

"What was it on the CCTV do you think that made Nick Lacey bolt?" asked Derek.

"Well, I'd put my money on it being Cleo. I think he suddenly realised who she was, which was horrifying as he was having a relationship with her," said Kate.

"Please tell me you are joking," said Derek.

"No, I'm not, I'm deadly serious," replied Kate.

"So, you think he recognised her and it dawned on him what a fool he'd been. That he'd been used, completely duped. It must have been mortifying, a massive conflict of interest," said Derek.

"Yes, I think that's highly possible," said Kate as she looked at her watch.

"I'm sorry, but I need to leave, I have a plane to catch."

"Harriet?" said Derek.

"Yes." Kate nodded.

CHAPTER 31

Harriet awoke from a deep, delicious sleep; as she stretched out her legs, for the first time in a long time they were pain free. The room was small, yet airy and light. White billowing curtains danced in the pine-fragranced breeze. She could just make out the sound of water lapping on the shoreline outside.

She wasn't frightened, the place felt calm and safe. There was a knock at the door and a smiling Kate entered carrying a tray of honey pancakes and hot coffee. She placed the tray beside Harriet and gave her a hug.

"It's so lovely to see you awake and smiling. Welcome back."

"Thank you, it's lovely to be back."

"Before you ask, Ben and Amelia are absolutely fine. They're happy at Annie's and I've kept in regular contact with them. You can face-time them in a bit, I'll get it set up for you."

"I would love that so much. I can't wait to see them and catch up with them. Thank you so very much. Any news of my father?"

"I don't know, but I can find out. I've been working with Derek Wynn and Mike Taylor, they might know."

"You have?"

"Yes, there's lots to catch up with but work can wait."

"What's the last thing you remember?" Kate sat on the edge of the bed.

"I remember hitting my head, but after that it's a blank."

"Okay, do you recall what you were doing in the vehicle?" Kate watched for signs of recollection. Harriet frowned.

"If I said you were engaged in a fight with Cleo? Would that ring any bells?"

Harriet shuddered. "Oh, yes. Did I win?"

"You did. Now don't try too hard to remember. I'm told there is a good chance it will come back to you in time. In the meantime, I'm happy to fill in some detail, if you feel up to it?"

Harriet nodded enthusiastically, between mouthfuls of pancake.

"After you were injured you were taken by helicopter to a small Surrey airfield. One of our company, a doctor at Great Ormond Street Hospital, initially attended to you before you were flown to Greece in a private jet. We were unable to guarantee your safety in the UK. You've received first class medical treatment but your recovery has been slow. To begin with you were placed in an induced coma. Ten days ago, you were deemed well enough to be transferred to this house."

"Which is where exactly?"

"On the outskirts of Kavala, the second largest seaport in northern Greece. In ancient times, it was a principle Macedonian seaport. Over the years there've been numerous border changes."

"How long have I been in Greece?"

"Getting on for two months."

"Two months? Really?"

"Yes, you were poorly. Now, I don't want to get in trouble for wearing you out so I think that's enough catching up for today."

Once again Harriet was alone. She reflected on events, unsure about how she felt. It was comforting to have Kate around and although they really didn't know each other Harriet felt relaxed in her company; she seemed genuine and kind. She estimated Kate was probably about fifteen years younger than her.

It was a cold icy November morning when a small party on horseback set off in the direction of the mountains.

"Harriet, we're off on an adventure. The trip is quite physical; are you up to it?" asked Kate.

"I most certainly am," said a smiling Harriet who was relishing being outside.

"I hope you understand that I cannot tell you too much, but you will learn more as the trip progresses."

They rode hard and fast. Kate was an accomplished horsewoman. Tall and lean, she rode with confidence and skill. For Harriet, it was considerably more challenging. Although she'd ridden as a teenager she estimated that it had been twenty years since she last sat in the saddle, but she wasn't about to complain.

As they wound their way up the hillside Harriet marvelled at the scenery: rocky outcrops, tall grasses, pine and eucalyptus trees as far as the eye could see. Slate purple mountains towered above them. In the early morning light, they might have been mistaken for ancient castle walls. It seemed strangely familiar.

They wound their way up an increasingly steep mud track. Towards midday their surroundings began to change, with dirt giving way to rocky uneven ground. Then, a deep dank forest. After they'd been riding for approximately five hours, Kate signalled to the party to stop in a sheltered clearing, where they tended to their horses.

A small wood fire was lit for warmth. They ate bread, a local hard cheese, spinach and feta pastries, olives, and of course the local wine. After lunch Harriet and Kate stretched their legs. From a natural clearing Harriet could see just how far they had climbed that morning. She could just make out the outline of Kavala in the distance.

"In the reign of Philip II of Macedon, Kavala was known by the name of Imathia. If you look carefully you may just be able to make out its harbour beyond that ridge." Kate pointed into the distance.

"It's breath-taking, the sky is almost the same hue as the sea, and cloudless; the air dry and icy. It takes your breath away, literally."

They walked on and found an ancient gnarled tree stump to sit on.

"Harriet, I want to thank you again for your bravery. Without your intervention we would have come to great harm."

"That's kind of you, but you don't know that for sure."

"I do. I felt so helpless, so naïve. I hadn't a clue how to get us out of the fix we were in, but then you came to our rescue."

"Look, no matter what state I was in, I couldn't leave you. I had to do something. I guess you could say I was the 'accidental warrior'," said Harriet winking at the young woman at her side. They sat in companionable silence for a minute or two.

"There's a rare and sacred place in the Pangaion hills, on Mount Pangeon. Its actual location is known only to a handful of individuals. It's a secret that has been kept for several thousand years. Early on, our survival literally depended on it remaining undiscovered. The route has been handed down by word of mouth over the years, and now is only known through the one remaining unbroken blood line," Kate continued.

"I belong to a secret organisation known as 'The Guardians'. The Guardians are the custodians of King Philip II's heritage, or his legacy. Have you heard of him?" Harriet nodded. "Philip was on the brink of unifying not only the Greek World but far further afield: Asia, Egypt and Syria when he was assassinated. Contrary to the view of some historians, he was aware of his own mortality and left his closest advisors implicit instructions should he die unexpectedly.

"It was Philip's decree that his legacy should be guarded by his female descendants. This obligation was to fall to the eldest daughter and pass from mother to daughter. Where no daughter was born, it would pass to the eldest son, to be returned to his first- born daughter. The duty could not and still cannot be declined.

"Today, there is only one completely unbroken blood line. It began with Cynane, Philip's daughter with Princess Audata, and passed to her daughter Eurydice, and so on. Princess Audata was trained as a warrior and consequently raised her daughter Cynane in the same way. Indeed, Cynane went to war with her father, as the eldest child. Over the generations this line has produced some truly remarkable women.

"As small children, we learnt of our legacy, where we fitted in the hierarchy. From an early age we were taught to be apprehensive of serpents, and to distrust those with an affinity to them. We were also taught that it was Philip's absolute belief that one day the world would be unified. So, we wait, and we keep watch."

"Incredible! As far back as I can remember my father's been fascinated with Philip. Can I ask a question?"

Kate nodded.

"During the investigation, engraved stone discs kept surfacing. And I just wonder if you know anything about their significance?"

"They were Philip's vision. Gold coins covered in a mixture of stone dust from Mount Pangeon and pine sap. When this mixture hardened, one side was carved with a sixteen-point sun. They were intended for his offspring, true friends and supporters. They were a way of identifying those loyal to the King."

"Fascinating."

"Philip's son Alexander, and his daughter Cleopatra, the children from his marriage to Olympias, were excluded from this however."

"And why was that?" asked Harriet, frowning.

"The simple answer is that Philip did not trust Olympias and therefore he could not be sure of their children's loyalties."

"This probably isn't the place to talk about work, but I just need to know if possession of these discs by our victims means they were connected to Philip or to his loyal followers."

"Yes, correct. You got tantalisingly close to blowing open the money laundering and protection racket run by Jack Peters and his associates. But such was Peters' influence that you were moved from Operation Eagle before you could crack the case. We had a vested interest in helping to expose the corruption. And unbeknown to you, worked hard to try to protect you. You see, we wanted the truth to come out but were forbidden by our rules from direct contact. We experienced heavy financial losses ourselves at the hands of this corrupt syndicate.

"I should explain that with Philip is buried astonishing wealth. It was his implicit directive that it should be used for good, to support those in need. Over hundreds and hundreds of years huge sums have been invested and then used to support the needy. Sometimes famine, floods, or other natural disasters; other times, man-made disasters.

Unfortunately, several Guardians were duped by Troy Manning and his associates into investing in a property development scheme in Canary Wharf. Despite all the usual checks, we were betrayed by some highly respected, high profile individuals, who were in the pocket of Manning and his cronies. When our Guardian investors realised what was happening they complained and were silenced. Troy Manning was a senior figure, but he got greedy and that was his downfall."

"Manning was also murdered?" Harriet asked. Kate nodded.

CHAPTER 32

As dusk fell Harriet and Kate were joined by a young woman who introduced herself as Timo. Kate explained her name meant 'Honour'.

"Harriet, we can talk again later but I'd like you to go with Timo now. Put on this cape, here's a torch. Timo has something to show you."

Unable to get the measure of Timo in the evening light, Harriet followed her up a narrow track. After about ten minutes they found themselves in a narrow valley. They continued until they reached a solid rock face. Timo beckoned to Harriet to follow.

They entered a small cave. At the far side was a dark recess. Timo placed her hands on the stone but Harriet could not see what she was doing, despite moving in closer. She followed through a small opening in the rock, crawling on her hands and knees along a damp, dark, narrow, tunnel. After a short distance, they entered a slightly larger cavern which allowed them to stand upright. They walked along a lengthy stone walkway, barely wide enough for a cart, until they reached a vast door that towered above them. The enormity of the doors took Harriet's breath away. They must have been 50ft high and were intricately carved with hunting scenes. Most striking of all, they appeared to be made of gold.

Somehow, Timo caused the doors to swing open. They entered and found themselves on another walkway, in a cathedral-like chamber; enormous, immense. Harriet shone her torch around the remarkable space. There were huge carved arches and exquisite statues.

Timo took her hand and led her to the left-hand side of the chamber. Harriet angled her torch downwards into the dark recess below catching a glimpse of something, maybe a figure. Heart racing, she looked again, this time allowing the torch light to rest on the figure below. She let out an involuntary cry. For there, directly below her, was a male, lying resplendent on a golden couch. His opulent crimson and gold embroidered gown showed no signs of age. In his hands, which were resting on his chest, was a golden orb, the size of a small melon and shaped like the sun, with many solid points emanating from it.

Remarkably, he seemed to be almost perfectly preserved. Harriet stood for a moment, trying to take it in, a wide smile on her face. She assumed that the conditions in the cave must be largely responsible for the lack of deterioration. She leant over the balustrade to take a closer look. He was, she estimated, in his late forties, with a full dark beard and thick dark curly hair. On his head rested an intricate gold crown inlaid with precious stones. Either side of him were personal items: a sword, a bow and arrows, a shield, and long spear. There were also several golden chests and four life-size gold horses framing his couch. Harriet squeezed Timo's hand hard, just to make sure she wasn't dreaming. Timo squeezed back. The two women stood in silence. Some time later Harriet reluctantly allowed Timo to lead her to the end of the walkway and out of the chamber, into several inter-connecting smaller halls crammed from floor to ceiling with gold and silver ingots.

When the two women re-emerged, they were met by Kate. Harriet hugged her new friend.

"Thank you, thank you," she whispered in her ear. Kate smiled broadly. They were led down the hillside to a campsite for the night. Neither Timo or Harriet said a word on the walk back.

The next day, the small group of women made their way back down the mountain. Kate broke the silence.

"There's someone else I'd like to tell you about. I suppose you could say she's an unsung heroine, you won't find mention of her in the history books, and yet she was key to the events that took place and is dearly cherished by the Guardians. She is ultimately responsible for our existence. Her name was Princess Philia; she was married to Philip's chief advisor Antipatros. She was also sister to Philip's first wife Audata and Aunt to Cynane, Philip's first born. She too was brought up as a warrior, and by all accounts was quite a remarkable character. A legendary horsewoman, whose skill with the sword was celebrated. She was fearless, but she was also an outstanding tactician. It was Philia who planned and executed the liberation of Philip's offspring and ensured they were kept safe from the clutches of Queen Olympias."

"Liberation?"

"Yes. Using the cover of darkness, the children were located and smuggled out of the Royal City. Later, a mighty battle took place between Olympias and Audata. Olympias murdered Audata, but was herself captured by Philia. Philia, perhaps surprisingly, showed mercy. But it came at a price for Olympias, who was forced to promise to never again raise arms against those loyal to Philip. She was also required to wear a tattoo of a snake on the inside of her left wrist. Since that day both factions, the Guardians and Olympians, have co-existed. But there has always been something dark about her blood line."

"I'm curious to know what ultimately happened to Olympias?"

"Good question. There are many differing accounts but I'm led to believe that eventually she was stoned to death by the relatives of some of her victims."

"Grisly end."

"Philia was honoured by the Guardians and presented with an intricate gold necklace, a pendant, an exact copy of the stone discs. At its centre was set a large luminous green emerald. Cynane was also given a necklace, but with a sapphire at its centre. Each legitimate child was given an identical sapphire necklace. Philip's children by his mistresses were given a necklace with a white pearl at its centre."

"Do you know how many children there were?"

"A little over twenty."

"Really? That's more than I had imagined. So, just so I understand, Philip's male offspring were given a necklace either with a sapphire or a pearl, to hand down to their first-born daughters depending upon whether they were legitimate or illegitimate?"

"Yes, exactly right."

"Can I ask which necklace you inherited?"

"I have one with a sapphire at its centre."

"And do you know who your heritage goes back to?"

"Yes, to Cynane, daughter of Audata."

"So you are from a royal blood line?"

"An exceptionally diluted one now." Kate was smiling.

"Can I also ask, is Cleo...?" Just speaking her name made Harriet feel nauseous. "... Is Cleo by any chance related to Olympias?"

"You have been listening. Yes, she's descended from Olympias through her daughter Cleopatra."

"Which means, does it not, that she didn't receive a necklace, but is also from royal blood?"

"It does but, again, it's very diluted bloodline now."

"Does Cleo know this?"

"Cleo is very clever and I think she suspects. She may know more than she lets on. But, unlike the Guardians, the descendants of Olympias were not as diligent at ensuring their heritage was passed on. Never underestimate Cleo. She is devious, jealous and psychopathic. She cares only for herself and is the architect of many wicked acts. She is a serial killer. Human life holds little or no value to her. Her temper is notorious; perhaps a legacy from Olympias. I'll give you an example..."

She paused for a moment as she remembered the story.

"It's said that during a banquet, a servant had the misfortune to spill an insignificant amount of wine on the queen's silk gown. In her rage, she struck him with such force that the poor fellow flew across the marble floor into a nearby pillar. The crack of his facial bones resulted in many of the guests crying out in distress. Olympias did not seem to notice, she simply returned to her seat and calmly continued her meal. Cleo has also been known to fly into a rage at the smallest slight. Woe betide anyone who riles her. Be careful, my friend. I would passionately advise against making her your nemesis."

The two women fell silent until something else occurred to Harriet.

"Kate, I've just realised Cleo is related to you. "She's related to you via Philip.

"Oh, well yes, I'm afraid she is."

"I wonder how one man's DNA could produce such polarised personalities..."

"I would imagine the answer lies somewhere within the nature versus nurture debate."

"Perhaps it's possible for certain extreme characteristics to be carried in our DNA and passed on through the blood line?"

"It might be one explanation for why Cleo is the way she is."

"Hmm, I'm not so sure; maybe she just had a troubled childhood?"

"No, I'm pretty sure she didn't."

"You know what else I've just realised?" said Harriet,

changing the subject. "Cleo has broken the promise made by Olympias never again to raise arms against those loyal to the King."

"Indeed, and believe me, she will be dealt with if she survives her injuries."

CHAPTER 33

It was the beginning of December and Harriet's thoughts had turned to home. She longed to be re-united with her children and her parents. The desire to sort out her marriage, to move on with her life, was also playing on her mind. On a more superficial level, she craved her coffee machine and toast and marmalade.

Kate entered the room looking uncharacteristically serious.

"Harriet, you asked about your father the other day. I have news. You might want to sit down." Kate took a deep breath before continuing.

"Your father died peacefully in his sleep four days after your abduction. It seems the blood transfusion provided only temporary relief before his kidneys failed and he slipped into unconsciousness. He was moved to a hospice, where your mother sat with him. He was peaceful throughout. In the early hours of the fourth morning he made the faintest of sighs and that was that. I'm so very sorry."

"No, Kate, I'm so sorry you were put in this position." Harriet walked across and hugged her.

"I'm so sorry for your loss."

"I'm only grateful that when Dad's time came it was peaceful and he didn't die alone."

"Your mother told me how important he was to you, that you shared a deep bond." With her voice breaking, Kate placed a hand on Harriet's quaking shoulders.

"Have I missed his funeral?" Harriet sobbed.

"No, I think the plan is to hold it after Christmas."

Harriet sank onto the bed and wept. Next morning, Kate found her in the kitchen, looking pale and distracted.

"Thank you for giving me space last night. It's strange, my head tells me that Dad is no longer suffering and therefore I should be thankful, and, whilst I am, I'm also raging mad. Mad with resentment and loathing for Cleo, who deprived me of precious time with him in his final days. I just can't forgive her. I'm not sure I will ever come to terms with it. If she recovers, I will do everything in my power to ensure she is sent to prison for life."

"You've been through an appalling ordeal and it's only natural to hate Cleo. My only advice would be not to let your negativity towards her eat away at you, take over your life. You have been wronged and, with time, I'm sure there will be opportunities to redress the balance, but closure may not come in the way you imagine, or perhaps would wish."

"Oh, my God, you are far too wise for your years," said a tearful Harriet.

On the 7th December, Kate drove Harriet to the airport. It was time to say goodbye.

"I'm so sorry I can't come back with you. But I need to stay behind, just for a few days. I've just found out the Greek

Government intend to start mining operations in the Pangaion Hills in the New Year. Surveying work has already started and I've been asked to assist with a legal challenge for obvious reasons."

"I completely understand, go! I'll be fine."

But it did not stop Harriet feeling sad that Kate wouldn't be with her on the journey home. She knew she still had some way to go to a full recovery and needed support. She was still suffering memory gaps and had begun to suffer anxiety attacks.

At Kate's request, Mike Taylor and Derek Wynn flew out to bring Harriet Lacey home.

"I can't tell you how fantastic it is to see you both. Thank you for coming to get me."

"It's our absolute pleasure, it's so good to set eyes on you again. You look surprisingly fit," said a beaming Derek as he hugged her long and hard.

"Hello you. I've missed you." Mike held Harriet close.

The flight back was uneventful. As the plane started its descent to Gatwick, Mike asked Harriet about her plans.

"Well, I need to spend some time with my children. I can't wait to see them, they've had quite a dislocated life of late. I also need to see my mother. Then, I'd like to come back to work."

"That would be great, but why don't you take some time for yourself and come back after Christmas?" suggested Derek.

"If it's alright with you, I'd rather get back into a routine.

I won't try to pretend that I'm fine, I'm not, and I may try your patience, but there are individuals who need bringing to justice and I want to play my part in bringing this investigation to a successful conclusion."

"Well, we could really do with your experience. I'm sure there will be no problem with you coming back, so long as you agree to take time out on bad days." Mike looked at Derek who was nodding his head in agreement.

CHAPTER 34

It was two weeks before Christmas when Harriet returned to work on the incident room. Kate was back in the country and now officially a consultant to Operation Chapel. It was Kate who accompanied Harriet on her first morning. As they reached the entrance door, Harriet paused, reflecting on the anxiety she'd felt at entering all those months before. Today however, she felt resolute and excited to be back. As she walked into the room she was greeted by enthusiastic applause and cheering from her colleagues.

"No chance of keeping a low profile then!" she said, laughing.

Derek lost no time in calling Harriet, Mike and Kate into his office.

"Morning, team. I thought we should all get together as soon as possible, there is much to cover before we can have a full briefing with everyone."

"There really is, Harriet. Perhaps we should start with why Derek is sitting at Nick's desk?" suggested Mike.

Mike somehow hit the right note and described how Nick had suddenly disappeared, as well as their theories as to what might have happened to him. As he talked, Harriet felt sure Nick hadn't committed suicide. Something must have happened: he was either forced to go, or he planned it. She considered him far too vain and self-obsessed to take his own life, there was no question in her mind, he was still alive somewhere.

"Do you want to know what I think?" Harriet asked, getting to her feet.

"Yes, very much," said Derek.

"He's alive somewhere. It's not in his nature to take his own life."

"I agree. Initial results from the recovered files from his laptop are most revealing," said Kate. "We found Nick had a significant gambling problem, he was in considerable debt and being pursued by some unscrupulous debt collectors. I'm so sorry, Harriet, but I don't think there will be much change from the sale of the family home."

"The bloody bastard, I knew nothing of the gambling. So there's no money left in our bank accounts?"

Kate shook her head.

"Oh, bloody marvellous." Harriet sighed heavily.

"Did you find anything else?" asked Mike, putting his arm around Harriet.

"Yes, it appears he managed to get his hands on a counterfeit passport. I think it's highly likely he's now abroad somewhere. We still have some files to recover."

"Good work Kate, keep me updated. Okay, we need to talk about Cleo now," said Derek.

Harriet's face reddened as she attempted to regulate her breathing. Kate spotted her distress and walked across to her.

"Cleo is under guard in a hospital in Surrey," said Derek

gently. "She will be moved to this county when she's well enough. Although now out of danger, she has suffered significant facial and leg injuries."

"It will be a while before we can speak to her. I understand from the hospital that so far she's said nothing, but she does suffer terrible nightmares," said Mike.

"She's not the only one," muttered Harriet under her breath. "So, there's nothing to be done now, we just have to bide our time?" she asked.

"That's right. We are currently considering her background and taking statements from family members. You can have a read whenever you want," said Mike.

"Let's move onto Jack Peters and Steve Smith," said Derek. "You may recall, Harriet, that just prior to your abduction we were planning to arrest them?"

Harriet nodded. Derek spoke about the arrests and then the subsequent murder of Peters in the court cells. Harriet took notes; so much had happened in her absence that she didn't want to miss a thing.

"Are you seriously suggesting that Cleo was responsible for Peters' death in the court cells?" Harriet was wide-eyed.

"Well, that's what we are working on, we are pretty sure it was her. We just need to prove it definitively," said Mike.

As Derek and Mike talked on, Harriet realised that Peters' death must have occurred whilst she was captive, most likely when Cleo had left her for a few days. Feeling faint and clammy and with her vision starting to go, she sat on the floor hugging her knees.

Kate rushed across with a bottle of water in hand.

"It's okay, I'll be okay, just give me a minute."

Derek called a break in proceedings. Half an hour later, Harriet had recovered sufficiently for the briefing to recommence.

"I'm so sorry about earlier. While you were talking I realised how close I came to losing my own life at Cleo's hand and it brought it all back." Harriet took a deep breath.

"There's absolutely no need to apologise, what you went through was shocking. There's no rush to continue, do you want to call it a day?" asked Derek.

"No, let's carry on, this is important."

"Okay, over the next few days I'd really appreciate it if you could find time to go through the Cell CCTV footage with Mike and Kate. I'd like your take on it," said Derek.

"Yes, of course."

"Do you remember Melvin Cook?" asked Mike.

"How could I forget?" The faintest smile crossed Harriet's face.

"Well, he tracked the elusive Craig down. Craig and his brother were arrested and have corroborated Dave and Melvin's account of events in Sheffield. They also confessed to their involvement in Poppy's death and named Steve Smith as an associate of theirs."

"Bloody hell. Did they say who ordered the hit?" Harriet moved forward on her chair.

"No, but Steve Smith did. Realising that things didn't look good for him, Steve decided to co-operate. When we seized his phone, Kate ascertained that Smith made a call to someone as you and Poppy left the incident room. We also found texts on his phone for later in the day which seem to refer to the tragedy," said Derek.

"Yes, and then it got even more interesting because when I re-examined Alec Brown's phone, I discovered some deleted recordings. Their content was most unexpected."

"Are they long recordings, or can we listen to them now?" asked Harriet, moving her chair closer to the others.

"Okay, the first recording is a telephone conversation between Jack Peters and Alec Brown. Have a listen," said Kate.

"Hello?"

"It's me, Brown."

"I trust your conversation with Wynn went to plan?"

"Yes Sir, Wynn was no problem at all, but..."

"But what?"

"Well I had a bit of an issue with Nick Lacey."

"What do you mean?"

"Well, Lacey was excited, he might even have been a bit drunk. Understandably, he was very unhappy about his estranged wife being dumped on his team. He threatened to make waves."

"You obviously dealt with him very badly then. Did I or did I not go through with you what to say? That it was unavoidable and would only be a short-term measure. But no, you obviously couldn't relay that simple message, you really are an idiot."

"Yes, Sir."

"Did you say he was drunk?"

"I said he may have been; he was loud, excited and seemed to be slurring some of his words."

"Interesting. So, how did you leave it with him?"

"Look, I didn't mean to, I don't know what came over me... Lacey just pisses me off. He is good looking, intelligent and incredibly well liked, and he winds me up."

"Oh, for God's sake, what exactly did you say, you moron?"

"I told him Harriet was being moved for her own safety."

"And let me guess, he now wants this confirmed at senior level and wants to know what we are doing to protect her?"

"Yes Sir, that's about it."

"Leave it with me, you've done enough damage. Don't say anything to Nick, but if he asks, tell him to expect a call in due course."

"This is dynamite." Harriet got to her feet. "Am I right in thinking this call was made on the day I was moved from Eagle to Chapel?"

"Yes, absolutely," replied Kate.

"I remember Nick complaining about a call from ACC Hillary Sellers," said Harriet.

"That would make sense, Hillary played a part in the deceit, albeit minor. It appears she was obligated to Peters for covering up a misdemeanour years ago. Every so often she was required to help him out. She's currently suspended but is co-operating," said Derek.

"I'd never have guessed she was involved," said Harriet.

"The second conversation is also over the phone and

between Alec Brown and Steve Smith. It's Steve's voice you hear first." Kate turned back to the recorder.

"*Sir, you need to report back that Harriet Lacey has developed a fast-moving line of enquiry. Despite my best efforts she has linked the death of Professor Grey to the presence of snake venom. I don't think it will be long before the other deaths are confirmed as having the same cause. It now looks as if Operation Chapel is about to become a multi-faceted murder enquiry. I think it's only a matter of time before other links are found.*"

"*I haven't a bloody clue what you are talking about.*"

"*No, but the boss will, and he needs to be told as a matter of urgency. So far, we've failed to find what we're looking for amongst the Operation Eagle exhibits. We don't know if the item we seek was recovered by Harriet's team or not. It's crucial that we satisfy ourselves either way.*"

"*Oh shit. Okay, thanks.*"

"So, Steve Smith was the mole. I thought at the time his behaviour was strange but I couldn't put my finger on what he was up to. This second conversation corroborates the recording Alec Brown played Derek in the park. It's clear that they were actively seeking Troy Manning's note book early on." Harriet frowned.

"I think you're absolutely right," agreed Derek.

"So, was it Jack Peters that Steve Smith named?"

"Correct." Derek nodded.

The room fell silent and Harriet's thoughts turned briefly to Poppy.

"There's just one more issue I'd like to cover today: Rebecca Wood. We can pick the rest up tomorrow. Harriet, while you were incarcerated, Rebecca's informant suffered the most horrific of deaths. Her body was found washed up on a small stretch of shingle not far from Tower Bridge. Her face was so badly beaten it was unrecognisable. Someone had gone to a great deal of trouble to ensure that identification would be a challenge," Derek continued.

"Please tell me snake venom wasn't involved?" Harriet was holding her stomach.

"No snake venom. But it did have all the hall marks of a precision assassin. Someone new." Mike was staring at the floor.

"Oh, my God. We have a good chance of catching the killer, right?" Harriet clasped her hands together.

"Unfortunately, not, the crime scene was sterile. We are really struggling," said Derek.

"What was the point of the murder? Do we know?" asked Kate.

"We've discussed this, and we think it was most likely a warning to Rebecca to stop asking questions and to back off," replied Mike.

"Shortly after the body was found, Rebecca was suspended from duty. We were all told she failed to register her informant. But I know her quite well, and I just don't buy it." Derek looked concerned.

"We might be able to help with that," said Mike.

"Did you find something?" asked Derek.

"Kate, care to elaborate?" Mike turned to her.

"Oh, my God, next time Mike tells me he needs my help on a simple job, please don't let me agree to it." But Kate was smiling.

"I have the feeling I'm not going to like this," said Derek.

"No, I think you might like the result, but perhaps not the method." A wry smile spread across Harriet's face.

"In the early hours of yesterday morning, thanks to Mike, I found myself in the Confidential Unit at Police Headquarters. With a borrowed 'Swipe Card' I managed to gain access to a stand-alone database in a side office belonging to the Director of intelligence. It holds details of all confidential informants and their handlers. I had to work in poor light to interrogate the computer, but I did recover several deleted files, which I copied to disk. I subsequently discovered that Rebecca did indeed register her informant, but the file had been deleted by none other than Jack Peters." Kate looked directly at Derek who had jumped to his feet.

"I knew it! Yes! But, how is this going to exonerate Rebecca? We can't use this."

"Ah, well, I don't know if you've heard, but there was a small electrical fire in Intelligence Office in the early hours of yesterday morning. It appears the Director's computers were damaged. When examined by Scientific Support, several recovered files were found. Let's just say Rebecca Wood should be back at work by the end of the week," said Mike.

"You audacious pair, you!" Harriet could not help smiling.

"Mike, next time I ask you to tread carefully, I mean it!"

Derek was frowning, but Harriet could tell he was feigning anger.

"Can I just say for the record, that being left on my own in that office was terrifying. All I could hear was my heart thumping in my ears. My hands were so wet with sweat that they kept slipping off the keys. I was convinced I'd be discovered. There's something to be said for an adrenaline rush, but not one that intense," said Kate.

"Point taken. I promise to be more sensitive next time." Mike was laughing.

"What makes you think I'll agree to a next time?" giggled Kate.

"What a day," said Kate, as she drove Harriet back to her cottage. "Tell me how you're doing."

"Sometimes I wonder if I will ever feel 'normal' again. I'm constantly tired, but I know my body's still healing. At times I find myself in a dream-like state, often I find I'm clenching my hands into fists or grinding my teeth. Although initially resistant to bereavement counselling, it's only taken a couple of sessions to learn not to be so hard on myself. I still have tearful moments, but I guess I'm getting there."

"After everything you've been through, I'd say your recovery is nothing short of miraculous."

CHAPTER 35

The second day of briefing started early with coffee and doughnuts. Harriet had forgotten quite how delicious they could be. Soft, light, spongy vanilla dough covered in icing sugar with a shot of raspberry jam. As she licked her lips she became aware of the others staring at her.

"What?" she said, laughing.

"I don't think I've ever seen someone destroy a doughnut with quite so much gusto," chuckled Derek.

"It was amazing, I don't think I've eaten one for ten years."

"No? Really?" said Kate in disbelief.

"Honestly!"

"No way," said Mike, laughing.

It was time to start the work of the day.

"Harriet, your call: what would you like to start with this morning?" Derek said, leafing through his note book.

"I'd really like to know if a girl I came across when I was held captive made it out. You see, I feel incredibly guilty, I can't get her out of my mind. I over-powered her in order to escape. I can't bear to think what Cleo may have done to her as a result."

"Sounds like chatterbox Alice," said Mike.

"Oh no, it couldn't be, this girl was mute," said Harriet.

"No, I really think it is. Kate found her locked in a cupboard."

"Was she badly hurt?" asked a tearful Harriet.

"No, but petrified," said Kate.

"What happened?"

"The first afternoon we were at Highfield Hall I found myself at the top of the house when I heard muffled sounds close by. I walked up and down the corridor, pausing every so often to listen, until I found myself outside a cupboard. The door was locked but there was a key in the padlock. I opened it cautiously and peered into the deep recess but there was no electric light. Reaching for my mobile and using its torch facility I had a good look around. At first, there didn't seem to be anything untoward but, as my eyes got used to the light, I thought I could make out a shape of some sort at the far end of the space. Crawling in, I made my way towards it. As I got closer I thought it was a pile of discarded bedding. I was about to exit when something made me stretch out my arm and touch it and, to my utter alarm, it moved beneath my fingers. I screamed, but curiosity got the better of me, and as I pulled the top layer away, two sparkling eyes stared back at me.

"The girl was almost naked, possibly in her mid-teens. She was filthy, of slight build, and very thin; her ribs were pushing through her taut grey skin. Her greasy shoulder length hair hung limply either side of her waif-like face. She had bruising to her arms and legs which were bound with electric cord. Try as I might I couldn't get her to speak. She was treated by paramedics at the scene and taken to hospital."

"That certainly sounds like her. How did you manage to get her to talk?" asked Harriet.

"Although reluctant at first, she soon warmed to my personality," said Mike, smiling.

"Really?" Harriet smiled back.

"Okay, no, but she did like chocolate. It was after the third bar that she just started talking, and I swear she's not stopped since."

"Who is she? What's her story?" asked Harriet.

"She's a distant relative of Cleo's. Poor girl. Her parents thought it would be beneficial for her to learn how 'a real lady conducts herself'," said Kate.

"No, you're having me on!"

"I'm actually not. Alice took an instant dislike to Cleo, and Cleo to Alice, so not an auspicious start. Alice was forced to work as domestic help. She was treated badly, often beaten. She lived a miserable existence. The only control she had left was to refuse to speak. Not even Cleo could make her."

"Do you think she would agree to meet with me? I'd like to apologise to her."

"Actually, she's already asked to see you. She's helping us to understand Cleo's operation. But you should be under no illusion she is terrified of Cleo. I'm sure there are more revelations to come. We are currently trying to decide how best to protect her," said Derek.

"I'm so relieved." Harriet got to her feet to stretch.

"Let's move onto Troy Manning's note book," Derek suggested.

"Harriet, it really was a bloody stroke of genius, leaving us that clue," said Mike.

"I just thought it might help."

"It was fucking brilliant."

"Do you have it?" asked Derek.

"Yes." Harriet bit her lip. "On the day of my meeting with Alec Brown and you, Derek, I was running late and shoved it in my desk drawer along with several other exhibits. But when I learnt that I'd been removed from Operation Eagle I completely forgot about it. It was only whilst I was imprisoned that I remembered the contents of my desk drawer had been placed in cardboard boxes and sent across to Operation Chapel. I'd put the boxes under my desk."

"And?" Mike jumped up from his chair.

"And wait a minute, I'll fetch it."

Harriet returned carrying an orange exercise book in her hand. They all gathered around. "Any ideas as to how to decipher it?"

"I have," said Derek. "Leave it with me for a day or so."

Just then DS Paul Jones knocked on the office door. Derek gestured to him to enter.

"Thanks for popping in, Paul. Everyone, I've asked Paul to talk to us about DNA, specifically a sample found on the forehead of Professor Grey," said Derek.

Kate shot Harriet a look of dismay.

"Yes, well, almost by chance we discovered a saliva sample on Professor Grey's forehead. When we looked at it, it was clear it didn't belong to him, so we set about testing it further. DNA in saliva come from cells in the inner lining of the mouth and from white blood cells. Through advances in this field it's now possible in some cases to reveal the approximate age, gender, race, and even sometimes eye colour of the individual concerned."

"And?" Mike was on his feet.

"So, as previously reported, we already knew from earlier samples that the donor was female and of southern Mediterranean descent, but we now know she is in her early twenties, with green eyes. What's not clear is the reason for it being there."

Harriet said nothing, but observed Kate pacing up and down.

"While I'm here I might as well also mention the tape recorder, you know the one sent to Superintendent Lacey?" said Paul.

"Yes, I recall, anything interesting?" Derek got to his feet.

"Oh, yes, I would say so. We finally got the chance to examine it in more detail earlier this week and discovered it contained a second recording."

Kate now had her head in her hands.

"My best guess is that after the Professor died, his tape recorder continued to chronicle events. There is evidence of an unknown female at the address desperately trying to resuscitate the Professor."

"Oh, God, this is so difficult. Okay, what I'm trying to say is that it was me," said Kate.

"What?" Mike had noticeably stiffened.

"I can explain. I was attempting to stop Cleo. I completely messed up. Arrived too late..."

"It's okay Kate, I've got this." Harriet placed her hand on Kate's hunched shoulders. "What I'm about to tell you must stay in this office, understood? If you feel you can't agree to this, you should leave now." Harriet paused, but no-one moved.

"You will need to bear with me, while I think of the best way to explain. We are currently engaged on a hugely complex case, it has many aspects to it. One of these relates to the existence of a secret Society which is over two thousand years old. Membership is not a choice, it's a heredity obligation. There are strict rules that govern how it conducts itself. Imperative to its survival is anonymity. Members are forbidden to have direct engagement with other organisations if there's even a remote chance that the Society's existence could be revealed. The dilemma here was that several members were caught out by a property scam run by Troy Manning and his associates. You may well be thinking, so what? Well, these members were attempting to invest large sums of money, not for themselves but with the aim of providing aid to the needy. To set up clean drinking water projects, source refugee camps, purchase food and medicine, and so on. When they challenged Troy and his friends they were murdered by Cleo."

Kate got to her feet. "I've already told you that I became suspicious of Cleo, but I decided to go out on my own, to follow her, and attempt to gather actionable evidence. But I was completely out of my depth, and naïve. I left my forensic footprints literally all over the crime scene. For my actions, I was very nearly banished from the Society. But I was given a second chance. I now have a wise mentor and I'm no longer the rash impulsive girl I was nine months ago. It was never my intention to cause chaos. I only ever wanted to help. Anyway, somehow I managed to persuade the hierarchy that we had a duty to assist. And that's what we've been doing since. I hope you can forgive me? And if not, I'm ready to accept my fate."

"Bloody hell. You are full of surprises, but I like your honesty and I sympathise with the dilemma you found yourself in," said Mike.

"Derek?" asked Harriet.

"Well, it's a lot to take in. I still have many questions, which I'm sure you'll answer in due course, but fundamentally you've been invaluable to this enquiry. Sometimes in difficult cases it's necessary to be creative, to work outside the box. I think we can say with confidence that we've done that here."

"Paul?"

"I'm rarely rendered speechless, but this would be one such occasion. However, don't worry, the whole thing is fascinating and my lips are sealed."

CHAPTER 36

The following day Mike, Derek and Kate met at Harriet's cottage. Mike was the first to arrive.

"Afternoon. Great tree. It looks and smells of Christmas in here."

"Well, that's because it is almost Christmas, Mike. You look different, but in a good way. You've cut your hair, ditched the mac, bought a new suit, and you're not swearing anything like as much. Come on, who is she?" Harriet teased.

"And I thought I'd been discreet. Was it the aftershave that gave it away?" Mike quipped.

"Come on, Taylor, spill the beans."

"Okay, okay, but don't say a word to the others, please. It's early days, but I've struck up a friendship with Annie Gittings."

"Oh, that's so great." Harriet clapped her hands together as the doorbell sounded and Mike put his finger to his lips.

Once everyone had been served with coffee and mince pies, they got down to business.

"Good old GCHQ, it didn't take them long to crack the code. Indeed, I'm led to believe that it wasn't sophisticated, but it did the job. Apparently Troy aligned each letter of the alphabet to a number; simple but effective, so my name, Derek Wynn, is 4518511 – 23261414."

"Can you run through how it works again?" Harriet crouched next to Derek and his note book.

"Troy numbered each letter of the alphabet, so A =1, B=2, and so on."

"So, my name in numbers," said Harriet, scribbling on a piece of paper, "would be 8118189520-1213526?"

Pausing to work it out, Derek replied, "Yes, spot on."

"Anyway, the book is full of names of high profile barristers, judges, bankers, politicians and CEOs. There are bank accounts, details of scams, the location of compromising photos and much, much more. Anyone like to guess as to the mastermind of all this?" asked Derek.

Harriet and Mike simultaneously shook their heads.

"A senior Cabinet Minister. I'm not going to name him. The fewer who know, the less chance of a leak."

"Fair enough," said Mike.

"Oh, good God," said Harriet. "Is there enough evidence to prosecute?"

"Yes, and I imagine it will hit the papers after Christmas. *'Government Minister charged with conspiracy to murder'* and so on... Excitement aside though, we must not speak of this to anyone. It's huge and needs to be handled with the utmost care if we are to be confident of successful prosecutions. So the plan is this: enjoy Christmas, and when we return at the beginning of January we start the complex and laborious process of compiling files of evidence to present to the Crown Prosecution Service."

"Derek, I really think we should at least attempt to speak

to Cleo before Christmas. There are so many lines of enquiry that we can't pursue until we have," said Mike.

"Mike, I share your frustration, but I would urge caution. Cleo is manipulative. If you are to speak to her you'll need to be incredibly prudent. If she can exploit a situation she will. You certainly can't go alone."

Harriet exchanged glances with Kate. "I totally agree. You've already assumed that she will want to speak to you. Believe me, she will weigh up whether there is any advantage for her to do so. She is cold and calculating," said Kate.

"Okay, I'm minded to let you go to the hospital, Mike, but only in Kate's company. You may talk to medical staff and get an idea of when she can be moved and when she can be spoken to formally. If the opportunity arises you can try to have a few words with her, just to get a measure of how cooperative she's likely to be. But under no circumstances are you to conduct an interview with her. All our dealings with Cleo must be by the book. We cannot afford any procedural issues or anomalies. Do I make myself clear?"

"Yes, and thanks, boss."

The following morning Mike and Kate drove to Surrey. They spoke to staff. Cleo, it appeared, was a model patient, nothing but compliant. But she had not spoken since regaining consciousness.

Cleo's room was situated on the second floor of the hospital. As they approached, Kate could see the blinds were closed. There was an armed officer just outside the door. The room was dimly lit, Kate could just make out an outline in the bed. Inexplicably she had a strong desire to flee. She took a deep breath and sat down, not wanting to disturb the sleeping patient. Somewhat absentmindedly though she found herself focusing on the figure in the bed. Something wasn't quite right, and it wasn't long before she realised that breathing was absent. The body wasn't moving at all. Almost at the same moment Mike jumped to his feet, having noticed the wall of monitors were eerily silent; they'd been unplugged. Pulling the covers back they found a female lying on her side, but it wasn't Cleo. Mike ran to the door to raise the alarm, then got straight on the phone to Derek.

"Boss, we have a fucking huge problem, Cleo's disappeared."

"Shit, what do you mean?"

"Disappeared, fucking vanished."

"How is that possible?"

"We're not sure." Mike drew heavily on his cigarette.

"How? When? Oh, my God. Harriet."

"Oh, bloody hell, you don't think she'd make straight for her, do you? There is a chance she's still in the hospital, they've locked it down to search for her."

"I don't know but we can't afford to take the risk. I'm on my way to her cottage now. Keep me updated, will you?"

Kate tried Harriet on her mobile, but it was engaged. A few minutes later she tried again, but it went straight to answer-phone. She left a message. Unable to focus, she paced up and down, increasingly frustrated by the lockdown. She tried to put herself in the mind of Cleo. Still weak and poorly, would she really make straight for Harriet? Cleo liked to be in control, she needed to follow a carefully worked-out plan. Kate tried Harriet's mobile again, but it went straight to voicemail. Might it depend on how impatient Cleo was to conclude her feud with Harriet as to whether she made a move or not now? It had started to sleet. The clock on the wall just served to remind her that time was ticking by and, so far, there was no word on Harriet. Unable to settle, she went in search of Mike.

CHAPTER 37

Harriet called Ben and Amelia in from the garden, for it had begun to sleet. Excitedly, they charged into the kitchen with their new puppy Archie, a black miniature Schnauzer, who looked more like a fluffy teddy bear than a dog. Energetic, bright, and eager to please, the children were besotted with him.

Before Harriet's mother Jane had left for America earlier that morning she'd handed Harriet a small envelope.

"Darling, this is from your Dad. He prepared it many years ago when he was first diagnosed with dementia. He made me promise to give it to you if I outlived him. I've absolutely no idea what it contains. Good luck my love, see you in a few weeks." And with that her mother kissed her tenderly and left.

Unable to contain her curiosity Harriet carefully opened the envelope. Inside were two pieces of paper. The first: a letter from her father's Bank Manager Mr Berry, dated the year of her birth.

Dear Mr Rayfield, I write to confirm that you have today deposited with us a sealed envelope, reference number 0086. Yours sincerely Mr M Berry.

There was also a copy of an official bank document entitled 'Safe Custody Agreement.' It contained the branch and sort code of the bank:

Customer George Rayfield requests the package identified as 0086 is held by the bank for a year and then after from year to year until the agreement is terminated· Termination of the agreement should be permitted on the instruction of George Rayfield·

There was a later addendum: *Or Mrs Harriet Lacey, nee Rayfield·* It was signed and dated by her father.

With some trepidation Harriet picked up the phone, but it soon became apparent that it was no simple matter to speak to the local branch of the bank. Having overcome the automated system, she was eventually transferred.

"Good morning, my name's Helen, how may I help you?" said a bright and breezy voice.

"Good morning. I'm an account holder at your branch." Harriet paused, "You know, this is a first, I'm not actually sure how to explain." She paused again. "Okay, I have in front of me a document which shows that some time ago my father took out a safety deposit box. He has recently passed away and I'd like to access the contents of the box. I do have written authorisation to do so. Could you possibly confirm that the box exists and that I may take possession of its contents?"

"Well, this is a first for both of us. I'm a mortgage consultant, but if you bear with me I'll seek some guidance and will certainly make enquiries for you," said Helen.

Placed on hold, Harriet had no choice but to listen to the piped music. After what seemed like an eternity but was in fact twenty minutes, Helen came back on the line.

"Mrs Lacey, I can confirm the existence of box 0086 which does indeed contain a package of some description. To access it you will need to bring your letter of authorisation and passport for identification purposes."

"That's brilliant, Helen, thank you for all your help."

An hour later Harriet was standing by the kitchen window with package in hand. The sleet was falling hard and fast outside. On the chalk escarpment she could just make out a stationary figure; he was facing the cottage. Glancing briefly at the man, Harriet turned her attention to the package in her hand, a red leather case about the size of an A5 envelope. Opening the lid with a trembling hand, she discovered a folded hand-written note. As she handled it a stone disc fell to the floor.

My dearest darling Harriet, do not be sad, for I am at peace now. Do not grieve, for it was my time to go. I spent many years searching for archaeological evidence to put this into context. I fully intended to publish my findings, but as time went on I changed my mind, concluding that it was not my place to do so. I now truly believe that some things are best left undisturbed. You have the distinct honour of being a direct descendant of Thessalonica, daughter of King Philip and his third wife Nicesipolis of Thessaly. Thessalonica was chosen by her father to be the custodian of his signet ring. It symbolises the legitimacy of his line to rule. It's now your turn to protect it. It is with huge pride that I sign out. With much love, Dad.

Hot salty tears rolled down Harriet's cheeks as she grappled with her emotions. Carefully she lifted a beautifully crafted gold necklace from the box. The pendant, approximately the size of a two-pound coin, had a sixteen-point sun carved onto its face and a large sapphire mounted in its centre. And, as described, she also found a heavy gold signet ring in the box, carved with the same sun motif and inlaid with a large diamond. She took a sharp intake of breath, reflecting that she was not 'an accidental warrior' after all. For now, it was abundantly clear it was in her blood, her DNA. For a moment, she marvelled at her heritage, struck by the realisation that with this legacy came enormous responsibility. She wondered if it had been her destiny, her fate all along? But her thoughts were rudely interrupted.

"Mum, Mum," shouted Ben from the direction of the lounge. "You've got a visitor."

Acknowledgements

First, and most importantly I'd like to thank my husband Neil. Without your steadfast support and patience, this book would not have been written. You are my rock.

Thanks to friends Ali and Jules Morris who showed such interest and enthusiasm for the project and who spent many hours reading early drafts. Thanks to Liz Hanlon for her encouragement along the way.

Many thanks also to the staff at Cornerstones, in particular author and editor Kylie Fitzpatrick whose mentoring was inspiring.

And a big thank you to everyone at Daniel Goldsmith Associates, in particular Lorena, who worked so hard to get the manuscript ready for publishing.

THE QUEST

The second thriller in the Harriet Lacey series,
out in June 2021

Cyrus Hart has uncovered a medieval bible amongst the personal belongings of his late Great Uncle. Whilst examining it, he discovers a map inserted deep under the leather cover. The map contains a symbol he recognises but can't place and a series of castles located in the Mediterranean and Middle East. His painstaking research reveals a distant relative, William of Hertford who lived in the mid- to late-1100s and was educated in the Monastery at St. Albans. In early adulthood however, he left the Benedictine Order to join the Knights Templars and travelled to the Holy Land with a man called Robert to join the Crusades.

Further research by Cyrus indicates that William and Robert were inseparable, fighting side by side for many years. They were highly decorated, respected by Christians and Muslims alike for their courage in battle. But, in 1185 they seem to have suddenly gone their separate ways. Unable to establish why, and convinced that the map belonged to William, Cyrus approaches Detective Sergeant Harriet Lacey with a view to persuading her to take some leave and to use her investigative skills in his quest. Harriet is reluctant at first, but when Cyrus offers to help her find out what happened to her estranged husband Nick, who suddenly and mysteriously disappeared, she comes on board.

Never far away is Cleo Morris. Filled with hatred and bile for Harriet, she plots her revenge and it's not long before she becomes a danger. But, she's not the only threat, for there are others following Harriet and Cyrus through Europe and the Middle East. As time goes by they find themselves in increasing peril. Cleo unwittingly gets caught up in the action and has to decide just how much she loathes Harriet.